looking for mo

looking for mo
daniel duane

■

farrar ■ straus ■ giroux

new york

■

Farrar, Straus and Giroux
19 Union Square West, New York 10003

Distributed in Canada by Douglas & McIntyre Ltd.
Printed in the United States of America
Designed by Jonathan D. Lippincott
First edition, 1998

Library of Congress Cataloging-in-Publication Data

Duane, Daniel, 1967–
    Looking for Mo / Daniel Duane. — 1st ed.
        p.   cm.
    ISBN 0-374-19083-6 (alk. paper)
    I. Title.
    PS3554.U232L66   1998
    813'.54—dc21   97-43486

For
Jonathan Kaplan
Reuben Margolin
Peter Reiss
and Peter Woolford
partners in an incomparable dream

In California there are no ideas. On the other hand, we may see God.

James Salter, *Solo Faces*

If you want to get to the peak, you ought
to climb without giving it too much thought.

Friedrich Nietzsche, *The Gay Science*

looking for mo

When Fiona first smiled at me, in the register line of a local café, I was too lost in thought about Mo Lehrman and the mountain we'd never climbed to make much of a move. For starters, I'd just found a copy of a book I'd always wanted to read: René Daumal's *Mount Analogue: A Novel of Symbolically Authentic Non-Euclidean Adventures in Mountain Climbing*. Hoping it might shed light on my obsession with Yosemite's great El Capitan, a perfect monolith twice the height of the World Trade Center, I stood there in the wood-paneled room thumbing pages when I should've been introducing myself. This in spite of having caught her eye once or twice in the nearby market where she worked, and having duly noted all those perfect freckles on pale skin, that thick dark hair at once well cut and sloppily worn. Indeed, I was so out of it that I said nothing even when she flipped to the last page of a paperback romance called *The Torch and the Tulip*, by Gwendolie Stonetower, the one and only supermarket bodice ripper I'd ever read. My ex-girlfriend Susan had cultivated a formula romance habit in college, and demanded I read one so I could at least tease her intelligently. She'd done her best to get through *Mountain of My Fear* (my favorite climbing book at that particular moment), so I'd yielded: love's whole hopeless mess, full of steamy fucking and barbarous men raping delicate, moral women, all happily resolved with marriage, money, babies, and slaves.

Although Fiona's peeking at the conclusion did seem a little against the spirit of the thing, I couldn't blame her for wanting to know how a love story ends. A lot depends on it. And anyway, what better conversation starter could I have asked for? But, like a turkey, I just paid for my coffee and brownie, found a table, and lost myself in Daumal's dismissal of all the great mountains of history as worn-out cow pastures, his riffs on Moses atop Sinai and Jesus' Sermon on the Mount, and his claim that the ultimate mountain should bond Earth to Heaven, offering a "way by which man can raise himself to the divine and by which the divine can reveal itself to man." I knew how much Mo would've liked the book already, and I tried to picture him just then, bicycling through the desert looking for surf. Already getting sweaty from that caffeine-sugar combo, I even imagined how surprised Mo'd have been to find that I still wanted to finish what we'd started.

That café wasn't really my kind of place, but it did help me escape my silent desk and silent apartment, my phone not ringing with inquiring editors, while my roommate Evan was pulling in a great salary and manifesting a functional adult life. It also offered sanctuary from the inexplicable restlessness that had plagued me since Mo had left, the inchoate pressure beneath breastplate and throat—an itching for something *more* that rendered me incapable of committing to the life before me. The tinted windows and dark interior, and even the September fog whirling up Golden Gate Park, all lent a cheap winter gravitas not only to me but also to the boozy-nosed asshole and the older faux artiste who sat together, simultaneously talking to themselves as if, in some fleeting moment of sanity, they'd agreed that, Hey, if we just do our things at the same *table*, people won't notice that we're actually lunatics.

Then I noticed a wiry guy blithely introducing himself to Fiona and asking if her name wouldn't happen to be Kimberly. He was pretty well built and had a roguish appeal, but Fiona just shook her head dismissively and turned back to *The Torch and the Tulip*. She nervously rubbed her faintly freckled collarbone, which was contrasted sharply with the snow-white tits bursting out of the Tulip's bodice on that stupid book cover. Those older romance cover illustrations are pretty well market-coded for smut level, and this one promised exactly the hot, detailed sex scenes that the story delivered. Funny, too, because in spite of her plain white T-shirt, jeans, and black canvas sneakers, she didn't look like that kind of person at all. She seemed out of her element somehow. There was a very intelligent vitality about her and a campy irony in her brown eyes. The book appeared to be only the kind of distraction you might get from watching a fire or an ocean view or, I guess, a television—just an odd literary bacon-cheeseburger in an otherwise gourmet diet.

And then that guy showed some real spunk, asking if maybe Fiona'd *like* to be Kimberly. She pleaded, "Oh, *come on*," but in a very nice, world-weary way that seemed to appreciate the comedy of his gesture. Encouraged, the idiot then asked which romance Fiona was reading, like it was the most natural question in the world, and not a come-on. I wanted to kneecap him with a table leg, but she actually showed him the cover and he nodded thoughtfully, as if the book looked great and had gotten great reviews. I'd recently developed a problem with staring at people—probably from trying to figure out how the hell they lived their lives. How they woke up every morning and just did it. Without regret. Without grinding their teeth or shaking with the strange feeling that they were meant to be someplace else, doing some*thing* else. I had to be careful, or my eyes would lock onto some poor woman's navel as if I were invisible and my gaze had no effect on its object, much the way children stare raptly into the eyes of mysterious strangers. So, blocking out the agony of this poor bastard failing utterly to connect with another human being, I covered my ears, started humming to myself, and finally just left for the men's room.

The unisex toilets were marked Sure and Unsure, and if I'd honestly searched my soul I would've taken Unsure, but I felt that surety was as much a matter of willed insistence as of biographical fact, and that admitting unsurety invited personal chaos. Nevertheless, when I reached for the Sure knob, I found it locked. I had to use Unsure after all, and it did have a certain flair, including thick crimson paint on the walls and tabloid articles papered above the urinals—which I appreciated, having a compulsion to sneak in text bites at every entertainment lapse. When I stepped out of Unsure, the rogue had mercifully disappeared and Fiona was marching off to the self-serve refills table. I was determined not to blow a second chance, so, reckoning my first brownie mere foreplay to the desired chocolate orgasm, and my coffee a little cold, I grabbed my cup and followed. From behind, I couldn't help noticing how her hair was messy in back, as if from a pillow, or how great her fine neck and shoulders looked in that white shirt. And then we were *at* the coffee table, and something about her—about my intuition that we'd have an awful lot in common—got me picturing how we'd leave tomorrow in an old sedan to wander the foggy coves of the great Northwest, merge dreams and identities as we picked fruit for enough gas money to make the trans-Alaskan highway, and do a season on Aleutian fishing boats while making soulful love nightly in our tiny seaside cottage until first snow, when we'd flee south and buy a shack in this little Baja desert town called Todos Santos. We'd pass another year there spearfishing, surfing clean point waves, and blankly watching saguaro cacti bloom after sudden, drenching rains. But I was in the midst of a monthlong fit of such escapist visions, and they didn't really mean much. Especially since it was my buddy Mo who did stuff like that—not me. In fact, like I said, he was in Baja even then, grilling hand-caught tuna on vast and vacant beaches and waiting out the flat spells between good swells. And I was probably just wishing I could be more like him.

When I started my ridiculous game of Just a little regular coffee on bottom, smother it with decaf, second thoughts, douse in a little more caff, add lowfat, but then weaken and decide to lard in some cream, Fiona grabbed a plastic lid for her cup, indicating "to go" intentions. I had to say something.

"You see any cream?" I asked, making my geekish Big Move.

She repeated the word: "Cream." Her very dark, coffee-colored eyes saw right through the question, and forgave it on principle.

Losing all peripheral vision under the influence of her gaze, I nodded: cream.

"Right in front of you," she said, grabbing a little stir-stick. She had some vague air of deliciously saddened compassion for human folly that got me thinking she'd be the perfect companion to laugh at my pretensions, cherish my flawed soul's potential for goodness, and render the metanarrative of my life an irrelevancy in comparison to the pleasures of each upcoming meal. So I asked what she was drinking.

Fiona smiled in an old-time starlet way that killed me. "You know what?" she replied. "It's one of those soy-carob-Cafix mochas."

I laughed. I hated that stuff.

"I've just always wondered why anyone would get one. Want a taste?"

Of course, and it wasn't bad after all. "Little trouble with that guy?"

She looked startled by the question, but then her face softened. "Well," she said, with a faintly ironic gleam, "he asked me out, which is pretty gross."

For a second, she looked as though waiting for me to speak, but then she waved with her fingers, said, "Well, see ya," pulled back the café's heavy oak door, and disappeared.

The morning after I met Fiona, a sunny Saturday with fog billowing just offshore, the water in my little Revere Ware pot boiled while the kettle screeched and the radio rambled about city council bond issues. I added cinnamon honey to some Earl Grey (I drank tea in the mornings because its caffeine seemed to metabolize less quickly than the caffeine in coffee, relieving the morning brain vise a few clicks without triggering the self-hating node of the superego), and then I put an egg in to soft-boil. Across the Great Highway and beyond the grassy dunes, roiling junk surf sloshed along the strand while the newscaster reported on a light rail extension for the South Bay, two fatal accidents on the highway, and a crack addict with full-blown AIDS whose girlfriend bailed him out of jail for their wedding. He'd pissed in a potted plant during the ceremony and raped his bride's eight-year-old daughter during the reception. The wife had been arrested, too, for allegedly beating her five-year-old son as he called 911. I couldn't listen to that kind of thing without getting miserable, so while the fog crossed the beach and tore apart on power poles, all that cool air getting sucked inland, I turned off the radio and put a couple of sourdough English muffins in the toaster. When my digital watch beeped dutifully, I cracked the eggshell and peeled it over the garbage. And, of course, flawless: white just solid, yolk still runny, the whole thing nice and hot between muffins with salt and pepper.

On the wall beside our breakfast table hung a poster of my worst nightmare: a storm slamming El Capitan. Eating those eggs and wondering how to start my day, I gazed at that grim vision from my recent past and told myself, I live here. I do. This is it. My time in Yosemite is actually over, Mo's actually in Baja without me, and I've got to stop imagining that authentic experience can be found only by climbing El Capitan. I've got to stop deceiving myself that, *Yeah, that'll do it. Then I won't hate myself anymore.* I mean, people have lived in apartments and accepted the world-as-offered forever, and they've known not to beat themselves up over it. And while I didn't know *how* they did it, I knew I could do it, too. Once I found a way to make the rent. Intending to turn my eye away from the past and toward the future, I looked out the window to where Mount Tamalpais loomed green above the Golden Gate freighter traffic. But in the process, I caught sight of the mailman. The long-haired, twig-limbed bearer of bummers was nearing our porch. Okay, in his hairy little hands: junk mail? Yes. Small envelopes? Fine. Damn! A big-one! I knocked over my tea en route to the bathroom, and was just reaching for the toilet handle when he beat me to it. He threw that four-pound package onto the porch boards before I could drown its all-too-familiar sound in the white noise of a comforting flush. I'd heard that heavy, three-hundred-page *whump*—yet another rejection of my Yosemite book—so many times in the past few months that I'd developed a Pavlovian response: a cold, disappointed sweat surfacing as my molars locked and my spine fell into a warped slouch. I sucked in a breath, stepped downstairs to the door, got all the mail, and threw the ninth returned bastard on the couch. That left only Sloth Ridge Press still considering my account of how Mo and I had decided that everything in life was phony except hard play in clean air, and had lit out in my truck for the Sierra Nevada. I guess Mo didn't really know I wrote, much less that he was my main subject, but I'd told the whole story of our awkward early climbs near Lake Tahoe, and then how we'd headed down the Sierra's east side to climb in a desert river gorge as if every short struggle could bring us closer to what we needed to know. I'd told how we'd imagined that, for all our lives, we would only want ever more barren, ever less populated places—perfect worlds in which boys would live in trucks on lonesome roads, eat lightly, and move well over hard granite and never fall. I'd tried to capture how, just when we were wondering why our hearts still hadn't come to rest, this mushroom-dealing climber named Yabber had said to us over coffee at a Lone Pine café, "You boys are just bored with little boulders. You need walls big enough to get lost on."

I'd been to Yosemite as a kid and had seen a million photos, but when Mo and I first rounded that road's corner with our ambitious new climber's eyes and faced the astonishing El Capitan, my whole body went limp. It was like we'd entered the Coliseum of the Gods. We moved right into Yosemite's legendary Camp Four, a tent-city mecca for climbers from all over the world. For the next few months, Mo and I thrashed up granite cliffs by day and drank with Europeans at night, talking over all the technical problems of the great walls of the world. We slept behind boulders when we overstayed our thirty-night limit, and we spent our little money on magic mushrooms that, in the deep space of Yosemite's off-route canyons, gave us the illusion of profound learning. We survived partly by grazing in the aisles of the market and partly by scavenging abandoned groceries from the Camp Four bear-proof food lockers—macaroni and cheese, old salsa, tapioca pudding, and anything else we could find. We also staked all our hopes for transcendence right where Yabber knew we would: on El Capitan, the great sheet of granite that flew highest above that overrun national park and all its human nastiness.

But the whole reason I was back in town was that I wanted to stop such dangerous doing and turn to the task of remembering. I wanted to give a shot at settling down the way Evan had—Evan, the engaged one, the one somehow capable of living among humans and functioning without this peculiar psychic choking feeling, this spiritual tightening of the lungs. The one who, as I'd been writing late the night before, had stumbled back out of his room, opened the hallway door of our linen closet, and pissed calmly and steadily all over his towels and sheets (I'd have stopped him under normal circumstances, but just then I was feeling deserted by his impending marriage). The very one who'd shaken out quite thoroughly, swiped at an imaginary toilet handle, and stumbled back into his room, where he now remained. Which was just as well. If Evan had crawled to the table, he would've whined, and I'd have been duty-bound either to make him breakfast or to share mine (I pitied his fiancée), and I didn't much feel like sharing. Which at last prompted the obvious insight: people don't offer sips of soy-carob-Cafix mochas to people they find icky.

Obviously, I was unemployed. I could have gone for groceries any day of the week. But there is something unsettling about shopping at, say, ten-thirty on a Tuesday morning. It smacks of recovery and listlessness. So, happy to join the working world's weekend meanderings, I drove up Lincoln Avenue, left the car at Eighth, and strolled past the enviably serene faces of the pink-robed idiots outside the Krishna Community Center. The indigent in front of Fiona's market looked so much like a bag lady in his scarves, skirts, leggings, puffy jackets, handbags and zero beard that people generally assumed he was a she, but I had a good eye for drag bag-ladies, as it happened, and knew he wasn't—he was a he, wearing the six clothing layers of his six personalities, and watching the sun spin and the fog swirl around all our frantic lives, beaming with heavy-lidded surety that even I, a cogitating young shopper, had a soul of lasting worth. So I nodded politely, entered that great market, and began to saunter through California's comical bounty-of-the-earth act, among corn cheap and sweet, fat melons, and bunches of basil you'd die for.

And then I saw her—the faint but self-assured hip swing suggesting that each step might be her last, and that it was actually okay because she'd been here before and knew everything would come out all right. As Fiona disappeared into the back room, doubtless donning an apron, I wondered what the hell to do—how to *carpe* the fucking *diem* and talk this urban adult woman into becoming a part of my new urban adult life. Not surprisingly, I also thought about how Dr. Seuss-like gangly Mo (as in mother, money, Moses, more, Mohammed, Mohawk, molybdenum, and especially Moira, the Greek goddess of fate, Mo my round-nosed, big-mouthed, unpretentious oldest friend) would have approached the matter. Ever since the day Mo came into my life in high school as an eccentric loner wearing a winged baseball cap, he'd advocated total abandon. Like with Lisa, this accordian-playing Yosemite waitress Mo met—afraid of nothing and as easy to be with as any guy. After a few weeks of fun with Mo, she went home to Seattle saying she needed time alone. Mo was bummed—he knew she meant what she said, but he also knew he really liked her. When he heard she was guiding a NOLS course in Wyoming, he decided to find her. Just to give you an idea of what was informing my Fiona-related strategizing, I'm going to drop in my recollection now of Mo's entire story, exactly the way he told it. He's the best storyteller I've ever heard, and any attempt to summarize or edit the yarn would only diminish an astounding performance and falsely imply that I had some role in its creation. So just imagine a wild kid about twenty-five, six feet four inches, with shaggy black hair and green eyes, telling you this over a beer at the Yosemite Lodge:

"Well, first, I hadn't ever ridden a motorcycle on the freeway before. So, man, going up Route 80 there were still all these gusts of wind, blowing me clear across whole lanes and stuff. I was pretty scared. But then it was great, just going seventy in my T-shirt with my little day pack on the back. And then, going up through the Sierras it started totally pouring. Huge drops and I'm in a T-shirt and jeans and the whole highway was just water and then I looked down at my arms. I was getting these big bruises all over my arms from raindrops hitting me at sixty miles an hour. Pounding me. So after that, I knew I could get through anything. But also, the bike started making weird rattling sounds. I was spooked, because I had a long way to go. I drove into the desert somewhere past Reno, way out this dirt road at night and slept there. Cooked up a bunch of grilled cheese sandwiches on the engine block because it was so hot. All I brought with me were a windbreaker and this really, really light-weight down sleeping bag.

"I woke up in the morning, out in the desert, and my bike wouldn't work. It's such a different feeling to be taking apart your bike miles from anywhere out in the desert instead of in your dad's back yard. But I had some tools. I actually had a lot of tools. I got it started again after a while. My friend had this house way the hell out in the woods and it was all surrounded by National Forest, so they may as well have had ten thousand acres. When I got there, me and my friend, and his sister and this other girl, we had to work on the house. Every day that's all we did. Shingling. Tar papering. Everything. It was great, and every morning, we had this wood stove with a huge cast-iron skillet on top. All we ate was bacon. Every morning we just threw in this huge slab of bacon, and we never cleaned the pot once the whole three weeks so it got full of this grease. And then we'd just throw like eggs and potatoes and stuff in the grease. It was great. Right before I got there, too, I called Lisa's folks' place in Seattle because I knew she had this break between guiding sessions for NOLS and I figured she'd probably be there. And she was, so I asked her if she had any itinerary for the trip yet, 'cause I said I might be in that part of the country, maybe I'd drop by if I happened to be around.

"She said she didn't have anything firm yet, but that she'd mail an itinerary to my parents' place as soon as she had one. Well, after three weeks out at this cabin, I decided to shoot out to the Wind River

Mountains to find her. On the way down there my bike started really screwing up, and I had to spend all this money on parts. So after that, and gas and everything, by the time I got to Wyoming I was getting low on money. Not even enough for food, really. And, right outside Cheyenne, my bike starts smoking. First thing I did, I went in and bought a pack of cigarettes. Me and my bike, both smoking. Blazing down the highway. But then, I had to fix the bike again. I had to buy a new oil filter and air filter and distributor cap and some other stuff, and then when I was back on the highway this bee flew right up one of the holes in my Levi's and got stuck under my ass while I was going seventy. Before I could really sit on it, it stung me right on the butt. So I had to get new jeans. Those ones were falling apart. And I had to get this Levi's jacket too, because with just my T-shirt and windbreaker I wasn't too warm. But then, there I was and all I had was twenty bucks.

"So I filled up my gas tank, then went into this liquor store and spent my last few bucks on a bottle of wine and a rose to bring to Lisa. I got some cardboard out of a garbage can and made this elaborate little protective thing for the rose and put it inside my coat. I kept it there the whole time. Then I called my folks up to get the itinerary so I'd know exactly where in the Wind Rivers she'd be. No itinerary. No mail at all for me. I couldn't believe it, so I called Lisa's folks, and they told me where she was—some place called Ragged Mountain. I had no money at all. Not a single dollar or quarter and

I hadn't had anything to eat that day and not even any credit cards or anything. This was definitely a one-way trip to see Lisa. I was putting all my bets on it. I knew if I didn't, I wouldn't have a chance.

"I went into this backpacking store to get a topo map of the area. I asked them about the best way to get to Ragged Mountain, because there were no trails or anything. They said, 'You can't get there from here.' They said I had to go all the way around to the other side of the range and walk like sixty miles, because they said this side of the range was all ringed with granite cliffs. Also, it's the highest section of land in the United States, where every single pass in the whole region is over thirteen thousand feet and there are tons of fourteen-thousand-foot peaks. I could tell these guys were lame, though, so I just said, 'Whatever,' and got them to make a copy of the map for me. Right then, I started walking. That whole afternoon I was bushwhacking, just trying to read where I was by the sun because I didn't have a compass and there weren't any trails. I also hadn't eaten, so I wasn't feeling too hot. Well, then it started really raining, and all I had was my jeans, my jeans jacket, and this windbreaker. And a down sleeping bag. No tent. No stove. I figured I was screwed, but then I found a cave. Never slept in a cave before—it was pretty great.

"When I woke up, I was really, really hungry. All I could do, though, was start walking. I had no idea if I was on the right track or not, and it was really hard going. I had to do some pretty scary scrambling and stuff to get over a ridge, and the map wasn't really making much sense and I was way the hell out there when I saw this lake. I was stoked. This lake was definitely on the map, and was pretty near Ragged Mountain. I saw this guy down by the water and he was looking up at me. So I yelled at him if he'd seen a big group of students. He goes, 'Yeah.' Pretty weird, because he didn't say anything else, and I got closer to him and he was still looking at me, so I said, 'Well, could you tell me where they are?' And he goes, 'You looking for Lisa?'

"I couldn't believe it. So I kind of thought about it, tried to figure out his tone, and I just said, 'Yeah.'

"And he said, 'Are you her friend from Cheyenne?'

"Oh, man . . . I kind of fumbled around, and said, 'Well . . . ah . . . actually I'm from California, but do you know where she is?' Turned out he was a roving NOLS supervisor, out there keeping an eye on the different courses. He pointed to this ridge way the hell off and said, 'See those little dots up there, that's her group. They'll be at Balboa Lake tomorrow. You can meet her there.'

"I spent the night down there with him, and he made me a little soup and some tea. The tea felt great, because everything I had was pretty wet. So the next morning I hiked up over this really brutal ridge, then way across this huge, high saddle between peaks, way above tree line at like thirteen-five. Finally I came down toward Balboa Lake, and there was nobody there. Nobody. I stood around for a long time just thinking, Huh, this is pretty strange. And then I decided to walk all the way around the lake, because it was really big. After a while, I thought I heard some voices in the trees. My heart was totally pounding at this point; I could barely keep my shit together and I must have looked awful, but I still had that rose in my coat. It looked great, you know. It was really blooming inside this little case I made for it. And I still had the bottle of wine. Even though I hadn't really eaten in two days, I hadn't touched the wine. Then, I saw these people who were obviously NOLS students. I could just tell. So, I asked if one of their instructors was named Lisa. And they said, 'Yeah.' I couldn't believe it.

"So, I asked where she was. This girl points over to some trees and says, 'She's back there in that blue tent.' So, I walked over there, and the tent was all zipped closed and everything and I didn't hear anything inside. I kind of said, 'Hello,' you know, 'Lisa?' Then I heard this kind of rustling inside and a second later the zipper zipped down and she kind of looked out at me. There she was. She looked gorgeous, but I don't think she really recognized me at first. She sort of stared for a second, then she was like, 'Mo!' And the first thing she said to me was, 'What are you doing here?' Like she couldn't tell. So, she got out of the tent and I handed her the rose. She put it in a boot that was sitting there on the ground, which I figured wasn't a very good sign, and then she asked me, the very next thing she said was, 'When are you leaving?'

What could I say? So I said the obvious thing. I said I was leaving first thing in the morning.

"Then this guy got out of the tent, too. Really studly Montana-type guy, obviously the climber hard-man. He kind of smiled. So they made me a little dinner, but not much. I still had the bottle of wine, and I wasn't feeling like celebrating, so I offered the wine to the two of them. I figured they could use it. They didn't want it though, because they couldn't drink while she was teaching. Lisa said if it rained really, really, *really* hard, I could get in the tent with them, if I needed to. I went off into the woods by myself with the bottle. I was feeling pretty lousy, so I drank the whole bottle myself, which was a terrible idea, because I didn't really fall asleep. The next morning I just got up and walked away into the woods. That whole day I wandered around trying to find another way out of the mountains, because the way I came up was actually pretty scary, and I wasn't up for it. I was getting pretty out there. Yeah, things were getting bad. I was cold and so hungry and now I was just getting exhausted. I could barely hike up hills and stuff, and I was just so worn out. I think it was actually getting kind of dangerous, and I was really, really depressed. It was pretty late in the afternoon, and I was like stumbling around, and I knew I needed to do something fast, because I couldn't go on too much longer. I needed food and warmth.

"I came around this little ridge, still way the hell up above tree line, and I saw a ptarmigan. It's like a bird about the size of a big hen. I just stood there looking at it. And it looked at me. And I knew, right then, what I had to do. I never killed anything in my life except bugs, and I never wanted to, but I had to. I picked up a rock and took aim. I was thinking about just hitting it right on the head. I wound up and threw that rock about as hard as I could and it went clear past the ptarmigan. Didn't come close. The bird started flying a little—you know, the way chickens do, where they can only fly a short distance. Suddenly, I wasn't tired anymore. My body filled up with energy and adrenaline and I was a hunter. Running, stumbling, jumping over rocks and bushes, I was chasing this bird throwing rocks at it. I was completely focused on killing this thing. Then I jumped over this rock and I was like five feet from it, holding this big rock and the bird was looking me in the eye. It knew I was trying to kill it, and I knew I was, too. I hauled back and slammed down the rock with the last of my energy.

"I missed by about three feet. It was the worst shot. And the bird flew off. I was so bummed. I wanted to give up and sit down. But I picked up a couple more rocks and started running again. Finally I let one go and nailed it. The bird started flipping over and spinning around, with like feathers flying everywhere, and then it dragged itself away with one broken wing and a broken leg. So I just walked up to it and broke its neck with my hands. Ray, I felt so bad about it. I picked it up, and it was so warm and soft still that I just felt absolutely terrible. It seemed so awful that I had taken this thing's life. But I put it in my backpack on top of my sleeping bag, and walked down to get below tree line where I could build a fire. It was a long way down there, and even tree line was still at like nine thousand feet—way the hell up there. Man, I was feeling so guilty. I kept trying to think about how I was going to eat it, and that it was okay; but that wouldn't work, so I thought about how I'd eat the whole thing, and not waste any of it at all, but no luck. I spent an hour building the best fire I had ever built, but still, the whole time, I couldn't get over what I had done. I even thought about how I eat meat in town, and as a meat eater I have a responsibility to know what it means to kill, but still, no luck. I thought about how I eat tuna, and I have a lot more to do with the food chain of that bird than with tuna, but that didn't wash either. There was no getting away from how lousy I felt.

"So, I went down by this stream, and out on a big flat rock with my pocketknife I cut the bird's head off, then its feet. And then I sat there and pulled all its feathers out and skinned it. By that time it was looking a little more like food and a little less like a creature, but I still didn't know if I could stand it. Well, back at the fire, I was starting to cook it up. I had a lot of meat. A whole lot of meat. And I was sitting there still trying to rationalize it, when all of a sudden an entire tribe of coyotes started howling right near me in the woods. Oh, Ray, what a noise! They were screaming and laughing and howling and baying and barking and everything else and I was getting really, really scared. I still hadn't eaten anything, and I was spooked.

"You know what happened? I became mortal. I'm not kidding, that's what happened. I had killed and was going to eat my kill, and the same thing could happen to me. I've never been so much a part of an ecosystem. Right there, when I realized that I could die and that it was okay to die, I was able to eat. I ate the entire bird, which was basically like eating a whole big chicken yourself. Every scrap. I slept really well that night. The next morning I felt great, too. I walked on out feeling a little better about everything, and when I finally got back to my bike, I called up my mom and she wired me a little money."

And that's the end.

I guess I knew even then that Mo wouldn't want me writing that story down. Otherwise, I wouldn't have kept my book a secret from him. It's just that it was such a goddamn good story—so much better than anything that had ever happened to me, or that I could ever make up myself—that I felt like I had to have it. Mo'd never use it anyway, I told myself, and people would relate to the tale's humor and pain, to Mo's willingness to let life carry him along. In fact, when Fiona reappeared, pushing a cart of fruit crates to a big bin, I was hoping to do just that—to go for it. At first, I watched surreptitiously while she stacked nectarines. Fiona mumbled either to herself or to the fruit as she put aside the bruised, saved the ripe for last, and lay each down as if it were alive and delicate and needing only a slight nudge toward its proper destiny. She didn't seem to notice me, and I hadn't yet decided on an approach, so I meandered among aluminum bulk bins that smelled of honey, soy sauce, and spilled vinegar.

"Hey," Fiona suddenly said, with total confidence, "it's you again."

"Skip those commercial tomatoes," Fiona said quite firmly. "These right here are the only ones worth bothering with. They don't water the crop, so the roots go all the way down to the water table and all the good stuff gets concentrated."

I laughed and put back the admittedly pale and thick-skinned industrial Romas I'd selected.

"It's true!" She was being playful. "They really are like fruit."

"You don't have to convince me—I'm a tomato freak."

She nodded. "They're kind of savory *and* sweet at the same time."

"Is savory really the opposite of sweet?" I'd always wondered that.

"Savory . . . I don't know. There's savory crepes, right?"

"You like crepes?"

"Much."

"'Cause I know a place, and . . ."

"I'm working late most nights."

I looked into my shopping cart.

"What do you do, anyway?" Fiona asked.

There was hope after all. Except I hated that question, because I tried not to mention writing to people. Too many guys say they're trying to write, and I was mostly just a guy who sat around filled with nameless dread. Which also isn't something you tell people. On the other hand, it was a good question, what exactly I did. I'd just spent the last of my savings to write my stupid manuscript, and I'd have to think of something else, soon. "Freelancing," I said, evasively. "And I write a bit. You?"

She looked around and we both laughed. Duh. "What do you write?" she asked.

"Just stories."

"True stuff? Or made up?"

"Mm, somewhere in between," I said, not wanting to get into it.

"You know, I actually make art, in my real life."

"Like what?"

"Useless objects. Paintings." She glanced toward the stockroom. "You want to know a secret, though? I don't really work here. I just worked here when I was growing up, and the owner's taking pity on me, so I don't go nuts. I'm only in town for a little while."

Naturally, I wanted to know why and wherefore, but it didn't seem like my business. "Well, look," I said instead, remembering a recent *Rolling Stone* dating article suggesting men ask women along on specific, appealing activities, "I'm going to Año Nuevo tomorrow to watch the elephant seals mate. Maybe you could come, I mean . . ."

"You serious?" She looked at me across the white onions.

I nodded.

"Elephant seals mate?"

"Of *course* they do."

She grinned widely, those dark eyes intent. "I know *that*, I just . . ."

"Hey, it's supposed to be a great hike, and, I don't know, you seem like the kind of person who might enjoy it."

"Oh, I do, huh? What day are we talking about?"

"Tomorrow."

"Sunday. I was going to go to church this Sunday, of all things. No idea *which*, needless to say." Her hands fell to her sides, each holding a nectarine like a baseball. "You're asking me out, aren't you?" She laughed, as if amazed. "That's classic."

Classic. "What's that supposed to mean?"

"Oh, I don't know," she complained. "I just . . . it's very *nice*. I'm sorry, I'm being weird, aren't I? Let me try again." She straightened out her face and in a formally courteous voice said, "I'd *love* to go see mating elephant seals with you . . ."

"Raymond. Raymond Connelly." Mating elephant seals. Unbelievable how the unconscious speaks, says the very thing you're trying hardest not to say.

"I'm Fiona."

"I know that."

She looked down at her name tag. "Of course." She offered her hand and I shook it. Said I'd pick her up right there tomorrow at noon. Maybe we'd bring a picnic. Then I walked quickly to the register with sweat trickling down my ribs, and ate three Enviromints in line (got the Endangered Species Trading Cards for the Kenyan zebra, the Philippine nuthatch, and the Amazonian piranha). Paid for my groceries and smiled widely at the indigent, nodding in agreement that Yes, indeed, the sun did spin all by itself.

All afternoon, I ran over the details of that encounter, wondering what Fiona's story was. I tried to picture her art, wondered which part of town she grew up in and whether we'd know anyone in common, and decided that, if nothing else, I was awfully attracted to her. And it wasn't just a physical thing—Fiona is beautiful, but that's not what gets you. It's this hint that the garden's neoclassical walls may be high, thick, and even topped with broken glass, but that inside lies a luscious wilderness. Indeed, I was so comfortably smitten that I didn't even go out drinking that night with Evan, who was enjoying a last prenuptial burst of social activity. He'd pissed me off by saying it was the wrong season for mating elephant seals—

that they'd be molting all their old skin off and would stink horribly. I guess he was just worried I'd blow another good thing, but it irritated me. So I decided to stick around and make use of those dinner-and-dessert tomatoes, maybe take notes on the last few days. I had one pasta recipe I could make in exactly the amount of time it took to boil the water and cook the noodles: While the water heated, I fractured the hiplike curvaceousness of a big bunch of elephant garlic, palmed the cloves into the butcher's block to peel their papyrus skins, and chopped the smelly meat into slivers. Then I chopped exactly half a bunch of basil, two of those tomatoes, four Kalamata olives, a quarter of an onion, a quarter of a zucchini, and three button mushrooms. While the vegetables sauteed in the garlic, I added the pasta to the water. When my watch beeped after precisely eleven minutes I threw the strainer over the sink, dumped in the shells, and washed the starch residue out of the pot before it had time to harden. Tossed the pasta and veggies in a bowl, sat at the table, and reached for the Parm.

Picking up my fork, I looked again at that photograph of my three-thousand-foot granite wall utterly dwarfed by malevolent black clouds. Though I never, ever wanted to experience a real storm on El Cap, I would have given a lot to be back on its sheer spaces. There's nowhere to go but up on a big wall, and the tasks at hand are totally absorbing. Day after day, you think of nothing but climbing, dealing with ropes, and getting to your bivouac ledge before dark. It gives life the kind of comfortable plot that normal existence never has. Mo's dad—this very charismatic guy with a silver ponytail, drooping mustache, and big belly—had climbed the Captain back in the late sixties, when it was still a big deal. He knew all the Yosemite climbing greats and lived this crazy bohemian life; travel magazines sent him wherever he wanted, and he'd written about every major mountain range in the world. But most important to Mo and me was this now-classic book Mo senior had written called *Scrambles Amongst the Sierra*, laying out the proper sequence of Yosemite climbing routes: a straight path to mountaineering enlightenment that took an acolyte three to five years. Mo and I had already destroyed three successive paperbacks, taking it as scripture that all the classic long-day routes—like East Buttress of Middle Cathedral Rock, Royal Arches, and the Chouinard-Herbert route on Sentinel—were necessary physical and spiritual preparation for success on the classic first overnighter: Washington Column. We'd felt frightened but earnest and committed on the great Northwest Face of Half Dome, which was the second real test of our ability to suffer and aspire. And we'd taken it as unquestionable dogma that El Capitan's Salathé route was both the greatest true rock climb on earth and, as if in a bad movie, a true journey into the unknown.

But I hated looking at that photograph. I felt taunted by it, and only left it up because removing it would've been a sign of defeat. So as I swallowed my last bite of pasta, I turned my thoughts to where they should've been all along: Fiona. Once again imagining her beside me, I was suddenly unnerved by how perfectly I'd calibrated my meal's volume, leaving me neither too full nor unsatisfied. Reflecting on the control required to achieve such an effect, I worried it would strike Miss Fiona, whoever she was, as patently neurotic.

But I needn't have worried. The connection between us that day at the beach was obvious from the start. Assembling our picnic established some common ground, as I insisted on red wine, and Fiona, upping the ante, added two cheap cigars. Once in my truck, southbound on the coastal highway, Fiona claimed to love being on the road, even wondered if she didn't need a colossal road trip at exactly this point in her life. I kept my Alaska-to-Baja fantasy to myself, not wanting to spoil anything, and after a brief silence, she asked about my past. I blathered about growing up in San Francisco's peacefully banal avenues, and discovered that Fiona'd spent her childhood over in a funkier part of town, near the Haight-Ashbury.

Likewise, I'd gone to bland public schools, she to very alternative private ones. We were only one year apart, and did know a few people in common: we even pinpointed a party we'd both attended. She'd left California after high school, now lived in Brooklyn, and was only out here for a little while—though, once again, she declined to explain why.

"Did I say I was a painter?" Fiona responded to my query about her art.

"I think so."

"Maybe I am. No, I guess I *am* a painter." She pulled her hair back and tucked it under the collar of her blue corduroy jacket.

"Bad topic?" I asked.

"No, no," she assured me. "Just, it's making me all squirrelly for some reason." She rolled up her window. "Okay, what do I paint? Think of something." She laughed wearily and put her feet up on the dash, right where Mo'd always put his. I drove across a broad watershed of bright bird lagoons, and the saltwater Sahara of that waveless gray Pacific seemed a less-than-farfetched metaphor for the unconscious just then, a perfectly peaceful sloshing about of the contented Oversoul.

"Hey," I said to Fiona, "it was just a question."

"No, it's okay. I do paint. I guess, lately, I've been sewing more—like, drawing with stitches, if that makes sense. I actually got two pieces in a group show next weekend." She rubbed her eyes as if to clear a mist. "But the awful truth is that since I got out here I've been a big slob." She sat up in the truck seat, took those sneakers off the dash. "Can we talk about you instead? Tell me what you write about."

As we passed a flower farm brightening the drab coastal autumn greens with rococo rows of gaudy violets, pale blues, and bright seafoam whites, I tried to dismiss it as a hobby, and not a big deal. But Fiona made me want to speak the truth, so I told her I'd written constantly since I was a kid, that I'd always known it was the only work I could ever enjoy, and that I was getting pretty discouraged. I'd had a few assignments for surf magazines, I told her, but the real thing was this big manuscript.

"You going to publish it?" she asked.

"I've kind of tried."

"What's it about?"

I usually didn't answer that question. "It's mostly about my friend Mo," I told her. "He's amazing."

"He know?"

The question startled me. "Mm . . . no. Why?"

"That just might freak me out, I guess, to think somebody was writing about me. Tell me the story though. Maybe it's not like that."

I didn't know one way or another, but I gave Fiona the basic version I've already given you: how I'd tried to capture those years climbing with Mo, looking for whatever the hell we were looking for. Her curiosity was a gift, and before I knew it I felt like an adventurous young artist instead of a clueless wannabe. She especially wanted to know why I wasn't going to try El Capitan again. It was too embarrassing to go into, so I told Fiona I'd gotten pretty fed up after our failure and decided to give up climbing altogether. Mo was gone now anyway—he'd biked off toward the southern tip of Baja by himself, planning to spend six months on a thousand miles of Mexican desert roads. Particularly noteworthy was that he was carrying a nine-foot surfboard on a fat-tired one-speed meant for coasting between your beach shack and the 7-Eleven.

"You didn't want to go?" Fiona asked, delighted by the vision.

Of course I'd liked the idea of dreamy months surfing ancient, silent beaches with my oldest pal. And the day Mo'd left on that bike, pedaling along San Francisco's vast Ocean Beach, I'd worried I'd never see him again. But somehow it wasn't the movie I'd wanted to be in. I couldn't jump from one fantasy to the next the way Mo could.

"You don't have to convince me," Fiona sagely and sweetly said. "I'm glad you didn't go."

Once we'd parked at Año Nuevo beach, Fiona and I joined the steady train of tourists stomping the cold and windy trail down to the hopefully barbarous love rites of a subhuman tribe with three-thousand-pound well-endowed males bellowing their way around supine, bemused females. It was nice to stretch my legs, and Fiona turned out to be one of those rare women for whom Levi's are flawlessly flattering, and to whom running shoes give at once a slight upward cant like that provided by heels *and* the air of athletic tautness. It killed me. As we walked, I heard about how that group art show—called Suture—would present sewing-related pieces in the back of a large truck which would, in turn, park itself outside high-profile galleries as a kind of viral exhibit. Fiona was nicely ironic about the "high concept" nature of the whole thing, but it was enough to keep her on the West Coast a little longer. She picked a little yellow flower and rubbed its pollen on her fingers, then told me she'd only been able to cope with working at that market again by taking the produce room cleaning chores: partly for the solitude, partly for all the great stuff you scoured out of the drains. "Something about how everything, absolutely everything goes down there and disappears." She picked up a round, flat rock. "You know what the deal is?"

"Tell me."

"The deal is that I"—with good form (her father's influence, as he'd apparently always wanted a boy), she threw the rock hard toward a small pine— "am pretty into wet biomass."

By a lagoon, three egrets spread six-foot spans of clean white feathers. I told Fiona that I'd scrubbed some wet biomass that very morning— our shower's grout—to the accompaniment of an opera CD.

"How corny," Fiona said, stretching in that dancer's way again. I got the impression her dad had always done corny things, and she'd loved him for it. She took a very direct look at me, furrowed her brow, and said with mock concern, "You're kind of a geek, aren't you?"

I grinned in spite of myself, feeling quite understood. The trail wound through manzanita and scrub pine, past interpretive signs that illustrated living things you might see, explaining how local mother mice birthed as many as fifty offspring in a year, making this Raptor Paradise.

"Geek's not necessarily bad the way I mean it," Fiona reassured me.

"But it's not true. I'm actually cool."

I noticed two hikers watching us just then, a black-haired man and a very short woman. Then we all four crossed dunes to the scene of supposed debauchery. A few younger seals bodysurfed the shore break, and hundreds of snoozing elephant seals lay scattered on the sand like dying refugees on an urban plaza. I didn't see a single barking bull, so I asked a woman in a tidy red jacket if it was mating season.

Most certainly not.

"Any chance a couple might do it anyway?" Fiona whispered when I returned from the guide.

I shook my head, smiling at her perfect mouth.

"Did you ask?"

"I can't possibly ask that."

She laughed. "Go on, ask."

"I can't."

"Ask."

So I did, enjoying myself immensely.

"Not in the way that would interest you," the naturalist said with a winning grin. "They're all females."

About twenty other tourists seemed moved to meditation by the sight of these things, and it wasn't so bad really. The females occasionally rolled over on one another, and a six-hundred-pounder yawned its broken-toothed mouth to let out a spattering belch.

"Can we agree on something?" Fiona inquired, as we found a log to picnic on.

"Yes."

"Don't you want to know what it is?"

"Mm . . . Okay."

"Don't get me wrong," Fiona said very warmly, putting a hand on my wrist, "it's beautiful here and it was great of you to bring me along, and they really are wild animals, but I'm kind of glad they're not mating *any*way."

"I know."

"You do?"

"Yeah," I admitted, "because then we would've had some furtive, allusive conversation about sex, right?"

She laughed out loud.

"I know," I said, laughing with her, "these guys are gross."

"But it is a glorious spot, Ray."

"Better than glorious. It's heaven."

"Okay, it's heaven. It's exactly what I needed, too."

We shook on it.

And that's when the black-haired man first appeared beside me. "I'm sorry to bother you two," he said with a kind grin, "but we have a bet. Here, I'm Carl, and this is my wife, Jill. We've been watching you guys, and you seem to be having so much fun together, but you clearly know each other really well. So, we've been arguing over what stage you guys are in your dating. My own theory is that you're still in the honeymoon phase—between two and six months—while Jill, on the other hand . . ."

She interrupted him. "I can speak, you know?"

He laughed, stepped back.

"At least a year," Jill said. "Just doing really well. I know this is totally weird of us."

"Two years today," Fiona said with flawless conviction. "Right, honey?"

I gulped, then nodded.

"Okay," Carl said, "Okay. I lose. As usual, Jill wins. Thank you, guys, a whole lot. Have a great hike and we'll leave you alone now."

A raven flapped over the foam film along the wettest sand as they walked off with their heads together, laughing and arguing. The fog breeze blew sand everywhere. Fiona turned away from the wind and lit both cigars. She handed me one, then sat down in the lee of a willow to open the wine. I sat beside her and played with the cigar, which was disgusting. Fiona kept hers bitten at the side of her mouth while she tugged on that corkscrew, but then she winced and spit in the sand. The wine also tasted crummy at first, but I gulped it anyway and chewed on the cork bits and stared at a black fin of sea-rock looming like a ghost galleon of lost conquistadors still searching for San Francisco Bay.

"A geek, huh?" I was trying to break the mood, get back to the casual fun of the moment before.

Then Fiona sighed, shook her head in self-reproach, and took a long drink of wine. She began cutting a loaf of bread. "I've *got* to be more careful what I say to people," she mumbled to herself. "You know, I recently told a guy I knew from childhood that he'd peaked in high school."

"Ouch."

"Is that mean?"

"Are you kidding?"

"It is?"

"Yeah, it is. You're actually a bad person."

"I'm a . . . Shut up." Fiona handed me a sandwich. "It was actually *true*, but you're right. He didn't need to know that." That raven leaned to pluck at a large live crab. "You like the sea?" Fiona asked.

"Love it. You?"

"Hate it."

"Why?"

"The whole woman-artist-drowning-herself thing —too out of control. You cold?"

"Why?"

"You're shivering."

"Look, I was just wondering . . ."

"What?"

"Well . . ."

"Out with it."

"Would it be appropriate," I asked, "for me to kiss you just now?"

She flinched at the question. "Definitely a geek."

"Well?"

"Maybe."

"Yeah?"

"Yeah. I mean, I have been waiting two whole years, right?"

"Just a trial kiss," I assured her, noticing Carl and Jill again, their backs to us. "No obligation to buy."

"Right. A sampler." With that, in broad beach daylight, we had a surprisingly familiar first kiss—a kind of soundless conversation.

"You're really shivering," Fiona said, quite concerned.

"I guess I'm cool."

And then Carl delivered that day's clincher. "Hey," he said, heading toward the return trail as Jill tugged at his sleeve and told him to shut up. "You guys? We just want you to know, you've totally, totally rejuvenated our faith in long-term romance."

On the way home, we stopped for steak sandwiches and red wine at Pluto's on Irving Street—laughing with increasing familiarity and talking through the mysteries of 1970s San Francisco childhoods, the madness of Brooklyn's artist communities, and, most of all, the impossibility of deciding what to do with a life. Fiona's family lived in an ornate Victorian that had been a silver baron's before the decline of Western Civilization, and late that night, parked out front, we kissed much longer than we had on the beach. Soon, it seemed ridiculous to remain in the truck, and Fiona made a fuss about how she'd promised herself not to invite me in, but said she now really wanted to, and would I accept such an offer? Just so we could be more comfortable, and with no guarantees of anything specific? She didn't want to wake anybody, so we crept through a large back yard in which someone appeared to be farming: row upon row of seedlings lay beneath clear tarps. At a big window, we took off our shoes and climbed into a bedroom frozen in the high school time warp that all such rooms are: in her case, an entirely white, 1980s minimalism now overwhelmed by the trappings of her artwork. Crates of cloth scraps and thread spools lay beside boxes of yarn balls and cheap little odds and ends like you'd get for decorating wedding cakes or dollhouses. Oil paints and brushes lay jumbled in shoe boxes, along with bits of wood for making frames. Over a fireplace hung Fiona's two pieces for Suture: a beautifully printed handkerchief with holes cut to make two eyes and a mouth—like a homey veil or shroud—and a little scarf on which Fiona'd stitched a remarkable likeness of a moose. On Fiona's bed, there was a single comforter, a worn-out stuffed animal I couldn't identify, and that copy of *The Torch and the Tulip*, its covers now conspicuously removed.

While talking until all hours about everything and nothing, and nailing down the distinction between savory and sweet, Fiona and I jostled around on the floor, from elbow leans to outright pronation. Fiona pried a little about my last girlfriend, so I forgave faults of Susan's I suspected Fiona might share, and complained vehemently about ones I felt certain she didn't. Fiona's answers to similar queries included a string of guys who'd treated her badly

(*Uh oh, better not be nice*) and revulsion for anyone like her father (except me, who apparently shared his geekiness in only the best way). The salient points seemed to be that, much like myself, Fiona had been spending a lot of time alone, and that she needed to stop doing things because other people wanted her to, or liking people because they liked her.

In a particularly long silence, I yawned to let Fiona end the evening. She admitted that she was sleepy, then added, "You don't have to stay, but you're perfectly welcome."

"Oh, hey, it's not that far, I mean . . ."

"No, I don't mind," she insisted, "really."

"On the couch, or something?"

"Like I said, *geek*."

"What?"

"What?" She stepped into her tiny bathroom and handed me a not-new toothbrush. My upper lip always itched when I brushed too hard, so I went into the bedroom. I was still brushing and itching when she threw her jeans in a big pile of laundry, put in a CD, and flopped down on the bed. Having just shared toothpaste, our mouths were a continuum of fluoridated mint, and we played around slowly at first, as if disinterested in the thing-itself, the point-of-the-matter: no freight train pushing out of the station, no avalanche starting to shudder (although inside me, naturally, the tidy ski village was doomed). Fiona's lips were slightly chapped, and she liked to prod in sensitive places, to tickle and pinch. Soon, we sorted out the difference between her gracefulness and my long-

limbed collection of bony angles, and then we began to blur the way you always do after twelve
hours of soaking-in another person's being—learning the contours of their shoulders as you run down
the corridors in their heart, and wondering at new
smells while musing on secrets behind their mind's
locked doors. Which is to say, in a roundabout way,
that we had a really good night, and one I still hope
to repeat.

My mind runs ahead pretty quickly. Evan would be moving out right after his wedding, and I spent much of the following week wondering if I could afford to rent the whole apartment by myself, thus making room for Fiona when she visited from back East. We had a date that Friday for an early dinner and a movie, and I daydreamed clear through a dentist's appointment about getting Fiona back into that bed of hers, hoping the same chemistry would prevail and agonizing over what to talk about and what to wear. When I got back at five, I found Evan home. Going solo to his family's Yosemite cabin that weekend, he'd left work early to pack.

"What-up, Chump-Change?" Evan said when he noticed me in his bedroom doorway.

"Don't call me that." I couldn't help but envy the way the guy functioned in the world, just going to work every day, getting down the line, and turning the chaotic specters of failure, embarrassment, dissolution, and loneliness into engines of early middle-class success.

"Sorry," he said, turning to look at me—a little man with a thick single eyebrow and mischievous blue eyes. "So?"

"So, what?"

"The girly. Tonight the night?" I'd told Evan every nuance of the Año date, and he'd gotten a kick out of it.

I told him that, Yes, I did have dinner plans with Fiona.

He nodded, said he personally was itching to lie around in the shade and swim in this river we'd all been going to since high school. "You know," Evan added, "Lehrman was just here."

"Here?" I looked around the living room as though he might still be sitting on our couch.

"Apparently he's been back a few days. I guess he lost that bike somewhere, and thought, *Jeez, me and Ray just got to get up El Cap.* He said he walked to some highway and hitchhiked a zillion miles—I love that guy—with like fifty pesos. It took him a week. When am I ever going to do something like that?"

My palms dampened. I stepped into my room and looked at my desk. I was relieved not to see a copy of my manuscript anywhere. "Did he poke around in here at all?"

"Nope," Evan said. "He just sat at the kitchen table staring at your El Cap picture. He mostly wanted to know if you'd try it again. Mo's classic, you know that?"

I noticed Evan had left the day's mail out—thankfully, there were no manuscript-sized packages there either.

Evan said that once Mo had crossed back over the border, truckers bought him fish tacos and microwave burritos and lined up his rides via CB clear to South San Francisco. Hitchhiking spooked me, but ropey-armed, Adams-apple-protruding Mo was one of those guys who could throw himself on the mercy of America and get nothing but love. You liked, trusted, and didn't want to fuck with him, and not only could he be anybody's friend, he *would* be. I couldn't believe I hadn't been here when Mo'd walked in. I hated not being the first to hear about Mo's adventures, and Evan never got them right anyway.

"Hey, look," Evan said, being a good guy. "He wanted you to drop by the squat tonight, and bring all your climbing gear."

Mo lived in a defunct school bus beached in a warehouse where these idiot performance artists lived. They called themselves Industrial Fright and Damage and built machines that killed each other. What do you do with people who put on shows named A Brief Excursus into the Black Hole of Eternal Flame, or A Pitiable Spectacle of Savage

Self-Abuse? I'd just seen an announcement for that night's show: A Mean-Spirited and Pointless Strategy for Perverting the Flesh of Animals to Profane Uses. They weren't actually idiots. In fact, they were geniuses. It just wasn't my cup of tea. "He wanted me down there tonight?"

Evan laughed out loud, and nodded. "What the hell do you have to do?" he asked, as I picked up a seemingly harmless envelope from the counter. "You don't work anyway."

"Evan, watch that shit."

"Sorry."

"I'm not kidding. I work like hell."

"I know you do."

"Okay?"

"Done."

"I'm going out with Fiona tonight."

"Well, at least go tell Mo I wasn't kidding about coming to my wedding. My mom even wants him there."

When Evan had packed his car and left, I noticed that that envelope had Mo's dad's return address, which made me nervous. Rightfully so, as it turned out.

Dear Raymond,

The editors at Sloth Ridge Press sent me your ms for an outside opinion. You will understand that I received it enthusiastically—looking forward to welcoming a new voice about the Sierra Nevada from a young man I know. But I must point out that quoting someone else's stories is a form of plagiarism. Sto-

ries live only in their telling—in my son's telling—and that telling is in and of itself a work of art. Did Mo say you could use his tales? Or do you imagine you have some claim to them?

Before giving the press my recommendation, I want to see if Mo minds being ripped off by a friend. Assuming he does, however, I intend to tell Sloth Ridge to continue their mission of seeking new voices by avoiding this one altogether.

Regards,
Mo Lehrman (Sr)

Walking toward the cedar-paneled sushi place where Fiona and I had agreed to meet (way out of my budget, but there's no better date food), I thought over the stories of Mo's that I'd used—mostly that long one I've told you, but also a few others. I mean, the whole point was that I absolutely loved the guy, so, regardless of whether or not I'd stolen something—which, I told myself, I fucking had not—I had to get to Mo before his dad did. Walking behind a band of Hare Krishnas chanting God to working stiffs and deracinated itinerants, I felt like a perfect candidate for their ablutions and wondered how my dreams had gotten so wrapped up in Mo Lehrman— from needing to write about him to the shame I'd felt over my inadequacy on El Cap. That's all it was on El Cap, by the way. After all that dreaming and planning, packing food and sorting hardware, I'd just gotten scared. We'd climbed nearly a thousand feet over the course of that first day—taking turns leading, struggling up those exquisite granite cracks and hauling our hundred-pound bag of supplies behind. We'd made fine progress on the greatest thing I'd ever tried to do, with the only guy I'd ever wanted to do it with, and I'd just fallen apart. Little things did contribute, like swallows slashing around my head and rats squealing in cracks, but the main thing was that I saw thick thunderheads boil out of the west, looked up into that three-thousand-foot browbeating jumble of overhangs, and flipped. Convinced a giant storm would come down upon us like an embodiment of uncontrollable destiny, I felt the edges of my identity expand in a personal Big Bang where the universe would explode from nothingness and then scatter until the end of time. I got all caught up in how we could get storm-lashed to that wall or fall a thousand feet to splatter on jagged boulders below. Heads popped like melons, every bone compound fractured, every organ ruptured. Where Search and Rescue would have to use toothbrushes and Glad bags instead of stretchers. No marriage, no babies, no more surfing perfect west swells on Ocean Beach sandbars. El Cap might have been the original stairway to enlightenment, but I'd suddenly wanted to quit, to trade in the story where honor demanded the heroic (fill in the blank with the war, polar expedition, or duel of your choice) for the one where the protagonist gets to come home regardless, his dignity unquestioned, and grow happily fat in the sunshine of his own back yard.

At the moment I demanded we bail out, Lehrman and I were wrapped half around each other's smelly bodies and dangling from a hundred-foot crack in the largest sheer granite monolith in the world, and I just told him I needed to go down, to quit our final adventure without really trying. He, too, looked up at those black-fleeced clouds, and he knew very well they weren't a real storm front—just an afternoon shower and some lightning, if that. He took a long breath in the whipping westerly wind and stared across the expanse of stone to the east, across the Shield and the Muir Wall to the great prow of the Nose. His eyes lingered where two Spaniards cried for help. Three Search and Rescue climbers had been moving toward them all day. With my harness cutting into my thighs and the thousand vertical feet below seeming far from an easy retreat, I watched Mo's round jaw clench and unclench. He began pulling our twenty half-gallon water containers out of the massive white haul bag that dangled there with us. A Navy rescue helicopter appeared in the sky as Mo removed the cap from each duct-tape-armored two-liter Coke bottle and watched its liquid ribbon spray in the Sierra wind. An act of finality—no point in lowering so much water weight back to earth, and once it was gone, no way to change our minds. By the time Mo'd emptied all but one bottle, that helicopter hovered just out from the Spaniards' perch. Then Mo opened a can of chili and ate it slowly with his blackened fingers. He looked down the Merced River canyon, across the foothills, and into the thunderstorms growing over the Central Valley, taking in the view as if we'd never be back. Mo chewed slowly, and gulped, and wiped his fingers on his pants as I watched for his mood; I even apologized in a pretty measly voice. He looked at me like we'd just met. Then his face softened and he said to forget about it. "No shame," Mo insisted. "No shame at all." And he meant it.

Waiting for Fiona at a table surrounded by bonsai pines, I drank a large sake and felt again all the stupid embarrassment of backing off that climb. People *had* actually died up there, like two mailmen from Fresno who fell six hundred feet when a bolt broke; or a guy who dropped sixty feet before his rope whipped him into the wall and sprayed his brain into a huge crimson Rorschach blot. But Mo had been utterly unafraid. He never seemed to doubt his immortality, or even understand that there was a future to lose. Which led him to do a lot of things I'd never have considered, like trying to get in a fight on his twenty-first birthday because he thought you should, or climbing unroped on frozen waterfalls poorly attached to their cliffs. ("It's not that hard," he'd said, when I'd asked, "not nearly as hard as riding down to gamble in Reno in full mountaineering dress on my Suzuki. I did that once too. Straight from the dorms with like two hundred cash. Blazing back I had this hundred-dollar bill and I went into a Burger King and ordered a Whopper with cheese and asked if they could change a hundred. The guy got this funny look on his face, went into the kitchen for a while, then he comes back out and goes, 'No sweat, they're on the grill.' ")

I meant to tell Fiona straight off that I'd have to go see Mo after dinner, but when she walked through the glass doors, she struck me as so beautiful—her hair up and showing off that fine pale neck, those dark eyes quite alive and her red-checked shirt and old jeans seeming the height of comfortable style—that I couldn't do it. I don't know that just any man would've seen her that way, but she killed me. Some aura she had of being able to turn on the sugar in ways that would make you forget how to talk. Sitting across from me now, she launched into a story about how she'd just come from a Gregorian chanting class at her old Catholic girls school. The chanters, apparently, had invited her to help build a church in the Baja desert for Sister-Somebody-or-Other. The notion had enormous appeal, she said, laughing at the strange midway quality of her life just then, at the weird (and, for me, quite enviable) freedom she'd given herself. Living and sweating in silent sunshine would, she felt sure, be a perfect way to get some clarity.

"And the drive down," she said, "—how fun!"

Before I could confess my own obsession with just such a drive, Fiona took notice of the planter boxes at our elbows. "My dad," she said, looking at those miniature trees, "literally reads nothing but the sports pages and the business pages—I'm not exaggerating. That's it. He may be the most boring person I know. And yet, all of a sudden, he's really into bonsai." She gazed around again at the little pines and firs leaning in non-winds off chunks of granite like a tiny Yosemite at our elbows.

I ordered another sake and thought about the particular dad on my own mind: Old Mo Lehrman. Here was this guy, I thought to myself, who could have just made his kid's best friend's whole life, and his impulse was to screw me.

"You know what?" Fiona said. "I want to tell you how my dad got into bonsai, because it's basically why I'm home right now, and I feel like letting you know."

"Deal," I said.

"My mom died a month ago," she began quite frankly. "That's not the point of my story, so don't, you know . . . Because she was sick, and we all knew she was going to die for a long time. It wasn't a sudden thing. But Dad drove home alone from the hospital the day she died, after dark. He went straight into the garden without saying a word. Still in one of his boring blue suits. He's never really talked to me much, but I guess I just thought, you know, that it might be the *one* time we'd have a conversation. My mom had just died, after all. But

64

not a peep. The guy's a piece of work. Me and my sister literally just watched *Twilight Zone* until we fell asleep."

At first, I'd heard only the tones of Fiona's speech, the inflections of tongue, teeth, and lips, but now the story captured my attention.

"I woke up pretty late the next morning," Fiona was saying, "with a big headache from all the crying and this stupid loveseat I slept on, and . . . God. I was filling the coffee pot, and I noticed something out in the garden, under this apple tree. I couldn't figure it out, so I turned off the faucet to look."

As she took a careful sip of sake, I got a horrible feeling. I wasn't sure I could handle hearing about her dad trying to hang himself from the apple tree.

"I couldn't believe it," Fiona continued. "It was Dad, still in his suit, which was totally ruined."

I put down my cup. "Oh, wow, I . . ."

"What?"

"Well, what happened?"

"He was on his knees. Planting trees." She looked at me. "What did you think?"

"Nothing. What happened?"

She dipped a piece of sushi in the wasabi dish, then held it dripping. "Well, I watched him until the coffee had brewed," she said. "He was just furiously digging little holes and stuffing seedlings in them. I opened the screen door and it was really cold out. The fog was in, and our neighbor's gorgeous Siamese sat on the fence, watching Dad. I would have given anything to be that Siamese. I had a cup of coffee for him, and for some reason

I couldn't remember if he took cream and sugar. Can you believe I was scared he'd get mad at me if I didn't get it right. Isn't that awful?" She put that piece of sushi in her mouth, and I watched her eyes water.

"Not necessarily," I said.

"No, it is awful. Anyway, my dad's still a really big guy and his suit looked like it was going to tear across the back. I could even see the scar through his crew cut where a baseball hit him a long time ago, which is a funny story." She seemed ready to tell it, too, but then decided to stay on message. "God, I wanted to talk to him," she said, leaning back in her chair and seeming nervous. "I put the coffee down on a root of the apple tree and . . . Do you mind my telling you this? I know it's a lot."

"Please."

"Really?"

"Be serious."

She smiled. "Well, I stood over him for a while and watched, you know? He just seemed so angry, troweling away. He never looked up even once, and he never said a word to me. He took a sip of the coffee, too, so he *knew* I was there."

"So what happened?" Somehow, I very much wanted to be the right kind of listener for Fiona.

"I went back inside. My sister knows my dad better than I do, in some ways. But she's so much older—she was off in college before he got really hard to be around, so she's so clueless about a lot of things. She just did what Mom would've done, and brought him a Reuben sandwich—he loves Reubens—and some cake, and she pretended it was all perfectly normal. Which was what he wanted, apparently. It was so phony. And then I flipped the next day, when he was still in the garden."

"The next day? How long was he out there?"

"I went and stayed with my friend Paz in Marin. The whole thing was too bizarre. But my sister waited for him." She dipped another piece of sushi. "Seventy-two straight hours."

"Three days?"

"*Fourteen hundred* seedlings—those rows and rows you saw in the yard the other night? We've barely spoken since."

It sounded so much like something *I'd* do: a whole private forest to lose yourself in, though you'd have to avoid arranging them in rows, so it wouldn't feel like an Oregon tree-farm. But if you did get your fourteen hundred bonsai placed right, with a pond for the sea and a stone for the mountains and a nice bench where you could sit in the middle of a knowable universe, it could be like a Pueblo Indian sandpainting where a shaman re-creates the known Pueblo universe in colored sand on the patient's floor, then puts him at its center, and there he stays for as long as it takes to reintegrate his world, to heal whatever discord has beset him. "That," I said, "is an absolutely staggering story."

"You think? You're the first person I've told."

"*Fourteen hundred?*" I'd completely forgotten where I was.

"I guess you're right. It's sick, too, though, isn't it?"

"I don't think so."

"You don't?"

"No way, it's beautiful."

She stared at me with unfocused eyes. "Yeah," she said, looking away. "You're not just saying that?"

I shook my head: no way at all.

And then the bill came. We split it, and I asked if I could walk Fiona to her car. Inhabiting the silence left in that story's wake, and the intimacy created by its telling, we strolled in the misty early evening past a store selling gothic sex toys and a movie theater showing *Wholly Moses* and *The Choirboys*.

Without explanation, Fiona began punching me lightly on the shoulder.

"Why are you hitting me?" I asked, as she took a third swing. We passed a very bland brick mosque, then stopped at a condemned building that had been nailed with a wrecking ball that afternoon.

"Punching," she said, inhaling sharply with a smile. "I think it's the answer to a lot of things. You know, just yesterday I had the day off, and I didn't know what to do with myself. I drank Scotch from about noon on. God, I'm glad no one was around the house. I practiced t'ae kwon do on the walls."

I laughed a little sadly.

"I know it must sound mad, but I just have so much energy. I think I'd be a really good person if I could find something to do with it. I used to run marathons—I couldn't get tired otherwise."

"Ever?"

"Not really. It's hard to wear me out. I don't sleep well, either. But, finally, around dark yesterday, I rolled up in a little ball and felt very feminine for the first time in my life. Kind of small and soft and passive. You ever feel like that?"

I hadn't really.

"Maybe because I was bleeding."

I turned to look at her.

"Well, it was only the second time."

"You mean your period?"

"My second one ever. Weird, huh? Puking and all that pretty-girl bullshit, and running marathons. Kind of put womanhood on hold."

The shattered stucco town house looked like the one I grew up in, and was a mess—the front wall gone and the roof caved. Fiona wrinkled her brow and looked askance at me. "I think I like you," she said. "You take all my weirdness in stride."

I laughed out loud. It seemed so improbable. "Think so?" I could see someone's upstairs toilet gaping in the streetlamp's hue.

"Think so. Even if you are keeping something to yourself tonight."

"Wait, you *think* you like me?" I asked. Pretty much the same sink/shower/toilet configuration as at my mom's place.

"*So* think. You're just very normal."

"But not a geek."

"Can't believe you're a redhead, though," she said, stepping back to size me up. "I just, if you asked me my ideal . . . it's pretty much the magazine guy: the swarthy, long-haired, dangerous type."

"The swarthy type—you mean like that freak from the coffee shop?"

"Not necessarily."

"How about me?"

She smiled affectionately. "Very dangerous."

As we kissed quietly on the pavement below dangling doors and third-floor toilets, my hopes soared when she quietly asked, "You know what I love?"

"Tell me."

"The way you can feel them *breathe.*" She inhaled the ruined building's dusty air of destruction like a mountain whiff of pine, then added, "Just kidding. You're not going to write all this down someday, are you?" Bringing me right back down to Mo, his dad's letter, and that very different story.

"Fiona," I said, "this is such a bummer . . ."

"What is?"

"You're not going to believe this."

She waited.

"I, well . . . I actually have to go."

She looked confused.

"You remember my buddy Mo that I told you about?"

She nodded.

"Well, he's back."

"And?"

"Remember you wondered how he'd feel about my writing about him?"

She nodded. "Not good?"

"Well, I just got to find out one way or another."

"Now?"

"I know it's bad timing after you just shared . . ."

"Don't."

"Don't what?"

"I don't need to hear all that. Just do what you're going to do."

If I'd known I could blow it so easily, I would've done things differently. I would've told Fiona right then how much she already meant to me and I would've tried to reciprocate her gift. But I didn't know anything, so I blithely raced out of her life, back home to grab my climbing clothes, and then crossed Twin Peaks and rounded Potrero Hill to China Basin. As I neared Mo's squat, my mind turned to the Captain's nauseating heights, to hard winds and sharp cracks and the lousy pain of infected hands making the morning's first turgid clenchings. I thought of sundries like knee pads and fingerless gloves, and of the sickening sensation of pendulum swings across blank acres of wall, even of the weird, dead sleep one sleeps on cramped little ledges. Mo's neighborhood was amazing, too. Here he'd grown up in a perfectly nice home, in which his folks still lived, and he had to hide out in a place where humans cowered beneath dead factories as if scavenging among the ruins of a civilization they'd helped destroy and now lamented. Shipping cranes blurred in the swirling gray sky like Trojan horses inside the walls of our now-vanquished city of Saint Francis, towered over echo-chamber warehouses. I slowed near a gang of Social-Realist factory workers etched into iron lintels behind a chain-link fence. In an empty field lay a ship's propeller entirely out of human scale, as if for one of those super tankers too large for any harbor, anchoring always in the distant deep while smaller vessels shuttled the oil ashore. Mo's building, the Angel Ironworks, took up two city blocks. It was a monster occupation of space that at first struck you as a billion-pound chunk of metal but turned out to be completely hollow, just girders and tin siding caging a lot of musty air.

A crowd gathered at its front entrance, waiting to see A Mean-Spirited and Pointless Strategy for Perverting the Flesh of Animals to Profane Uses in the Industrial Fright and Damage show space. That stuff really spooked me, so I drove around back and stopped in front of a gigantic steel door. Across the street, two brothers serviced a metallic gold Mercedes-Benz. As I stepped out of the truck, a loose-limbed can collector with a cocky-angled cap rattled his shopping cart through the ambient glimmer of the bay. The mechanics' pit bull didn't even stand up—from its bed of smoldering malevolence, dreaming of dismembering chihuahuas, it smelled can collector and was airborne before it awoke. The way you or I might find ourselves halfway to the bathroom at night, the pit bull found itself soaring across the oil-stained asphalt and, twenty feet out, hitting the limit of its chain, flipping over backwards and lying choking among paper cups and dead grass.

The collector sneered, put his globular nose into the air: "Motherfucker best watch that shit."

Hm? The nearest mechanic looked curious, unmoved.

"I just might have a pistol—you never know."

At a small door beside the huge one, I let myself into the echo-chamber emptiness of a dark girdered cavern. There in the shadowed silence lay the wheelless school bus from my childhood district that was now Mo's home. Near a pile of shattered desk chairs and demolished wall partitions, a chest of drawers stood in the industrial vastness. A few books sat on top: mostly about dune buggy construction and motorcycle mechanics (though not *Zen and the Art of Motorcycle Maintenance*, which Mo swore to be full of bad technical advice). I noticed with astonishment that Mo'd gotten his Brewer 9'6" single-fin clear back here with him: the big longboard lay across two sawhorses with a patch of freshly resined fiberglass bristling along one rail. It made me doubly sad I hadn't gone to Baja.

"So?" Mo asked, stepping out of the bus with a slab of bacon in one hand. I was thrilled to see him, and he was smiling expectantly, even bashfully. He reached out with his free hand and we hugged hard the way we always did. Maybe he hadn't seen my book.

"So?" I asked, too, stepping back. "Howzit?"

"Hear you met a girl." Mo seemed delighted for me.

"I met a girl."

"Evan says you won't shut up about her. She pretty cute?" Mo looked a little worn down, but tanned and nutty and genuinely curious about my life.

"Yeah, she's pretty cute. You should've heard this story she just told me."

"Yeah?"

I shook my head and wondered where to begin. And then, for some reason, decided I should keep it to myself.

Mo squirmed a little, peeled a strip of blubber away from the bacon and slurped it like a noodle.

"Little bacon, huh?" I asked.

"Yeah, lil' bacon. Diet of the ancients." He laughed out loud. Mo had some ridiculous yarn swilling around inside him, and we both knew it, so I opened a warm can of beer and waited. Soon a tidbit came out about how he'd dropped in on some endurance-running vegan friends of ours in Santa Cruz. "Amy bought a big Safeway soup bone for the local dog," Mo told me with his head bobbing and his green eyes scanning another strip of fried pork belly, "and she sent this guy out to feed him—that skinny kid named Bree, you remember him. It was so funny, Ray. He was gone really long, and then Amy goes out there and finds him on a lawn chair and after ten years of being a vegetarian he's gnawing away at this bone, gnashing his teeth and slurping marrow and everything. The worst part was that dog. It was kind of whimpering in the grass. Kind of staring at Bree and feeling depressed and cheated and shitty, like maybe he should try to come back as a human in his next life." Mo finished off his last flesh strip, sucking a ribbon of pig lard away from the pig muscle.

I noticed two stacks of canned foods like we'd taken on the Big Stone last time: chilies and tamales and terrible canned pastas; even the fruit cocktails we'd brought as desserts. All our crates of climbing gear were stacked together, ready to go. My palms dampened at the sight.

Mo saw where I was looking. "Go for it, huh?"

I nodded, and then gulped. "You'd really try again?"

"Sure. Soon."

I breathed deeply, tried to understand what Mo was after. El Cap had always been more my problem than his. "How soon?"

"I already bought food and we still got all the water bottles. We don't really need anything."

I could feel Mo's confidence again. Took another deep breath, looked around the warehouse.

"Come on, man. I'll even drive up tonight," Mo said. "You could sleep in the car, and we could stop over at the river so we'd be there for a morning swim."

Without conviction, I said, Sure, I'd try again. I guess I imagined we'd wait until we were refamiliarized before I brought up his dad and the book. I walked back outside to bring the truck in for loading, sat for a while before turning over the engine. I let my eye wander down the cracked sidewalk and wondered if I was doing the right thing—if I shouldn't just turn around and find Fiona, apologize for leaving her like that.

Mo opened the huge roll-up door. I turned the truck's ignition and drove inside the warehouse, stopping next to his bus. I dropped the tailgate, opened the camper shell, and cleared out garbage to make room.

"You get waves?" I asked, sliding the first crate of hardware into the truck.

"Yeah, I got some fun ones. Nothing insane. I got Rincon okay, and little peelers at T-Street, and Sunset Cliffs. And then I got San Miguel insane for like an hour."

"How about the beach cruiser?" I shoved our three snake-patterned kernmantle ropes, our harnesses, and our jumar ascension clamps into our haul bag.

"The bike was fine," Mo said, "except in big winds."

One thing was missing from the pile of gear: my old Tao climbing shoes, the specialized leather and rubber slippers that can lock into granite cracks and stick like glue to low-angle slabs. Mine had once belonged to a Camp Four climbing bum named Raffi, who'd spent the last twenty-five years toiling in outer space—a vertical ascetic whose climbing had become a mystical martial art. I'd never actually met the guy, but I'd heard a lot about him.

"Yeah," Mo said, "that longboard's like a sail." He'd stopped at some place near Pismo, he said, called the Road Kill Bar & Grill: You Kill 'em, We Grill 'em. "Three guys at the bar all named Frank," Mo continued, "and they all wanted to be a big fish in a small pond."

With all the ropes, carabiners, and protective hardware in the truck, we started filling all those plastic Coke bottles once again. At a gallon each per day, over five days, at eight pounds per gallon, we'd be hauling eighty pounds of water alone. Such a gigantic wall, really. There's no way you can take in the Big Stone all at once: if you're close enough to touch its smooth solidity you can only see a millionth of its surface area, and if you're far enough away to see the whole thing—like from an airplane—you can easily underestimate its size.

I asked what happened next at the Road Kill Bar & Grill.

"One Frank wanted to be a lawyer," Mo said, pulling apart a knot in the dynamic rope in his hands. "I guess in his hometown in Louisiana. The second Frank wanted his own roadside bar. The third Frank just wanted a woman who respected him." Mo took a handful of aspirin from his shirt pocket and swallowed them with a gulp of water. "I got into gambling with them, you know, playing blackjack? But I only had forty dollars."

"And?" As Mo filled the water bottles, I loaded them into the truck.

"Pretty late, I passed out in the alley with a six-pack of take-homes the bartender gave me. I thought I'd only lost twenty of my last forty bucks. I thought those Franks were all my friends. You know what?"

I could guess.

"I woke up by the Dumpster, still hammered." Mo lifted a crate of canned food off the floor, and slid it into the truck.

"Oh, no."

"Yeah, I look in my wallet and, sure enough."

"Everything's gone?"

"No, I'm *up* twenty bucks." He grinned as if still standing in the Central Californian heat, discovering the boon. So I grinned, too, as Mo sorted through his personal gear—his own climbing shoes, harness, clothes, and sleeping bag.

"Mo, what happened to your bike, though? In the end?"

"I got a little chicken and a rooster."

"Chickens."

"Yeah, chickies. I saved them from one of those big factory farms. I kept them in a milk crate on the back, except the rooster'd crow when I went down big hills."

"Mo," I asked, getting a little agitated, "why the hell'd you have chickens on your bike?"

"For eggs and all." He didn't even look up, just kept fussing around in the haul bag. Mo's heart wasn't in the story, and it was then I knew that he'd seen the book.

"Eggs, Mo?" I asked, getting nervous.

"Yeah, the chickies were too cute to eat. But the hen didn't really lay eggs either. My mom thinks she was too scared. I had to get off the bike every half hour and let them walk around, so they wouldn't die." Mo stood up now. "When I crossed the border, and I was passing through these little Mexican towns—man I loved those chickies—I pulled over to sleep in this field, and it turned out to be kind of a swamp. The bike started sinking." The setting sun magnified the high warehouse windows into hundreds of glowing plates, and Mo said he'd been getting ready to haul the bike up when a big horned beast charged out of the bushes at him.

"For heaven's sake, Mo. Horns?"

"I pretty much spent the night up in a tree."

"The whole night? You mean a wild pig."

"Watching this horned beast eat my chickies."

"And that was it?"

Mo looked at me as if another thought had crossed his mind. "Look," he said, "I was mostly thinking about the Big Stone."

"Yeah?" I was shaking.

"Yeah. We kind of got to get up it."

"We do, huh?"

"Yeah, we really do."

I took a deep breath, added a bag of nylon cord to the truck's considerable load. "You got any idea why, though?"

He laughed. "Pretty big, I guess. That what you mean?"

It wasn't, but I figured it would do. We both looked around Mo's space, mentally sorted through the gear we'd packed. "That's everything, huh?"

"We could just drive as far as the river tonight," Mo said again. "I want to stop there anyway."

"I can't believe we're really going to do this. It's fucking great." And then I remembered. "Wait, Mo," I said, getting worried. "You know what? I don't see my climbing shoes."

Mo seemed nervous as he led me down a long corridor. Near the last vestige of the defunct ironworks, where hundreds of manhole covers lay on wooden racks, Mo stopped at the backstage entrance to the Industrial Fright and Damage machine shop.

"Mo," I said, "don't make me go in there. That shit's dangerous."

"Raymond, relax." He opened the door. And, of course, I followed him through it. The workshop was, as it had always been, cluttered with power tools and racks of scavenged metal and machine parts attended by that small army of earnest young anarchists lost in grease-monkey end-of-the-world fantasies. A bald woman in leather pants touched up a life-size, papier-mâché apostle Paul, while a six-foot-six bald guy with droopy eyes stapled a lamb shank and goat's head onto a robot that Mo told me would walk and quiver and smell like a good argument for cremation.

I hated that crap. "My shoes are in here?" I asked. "Those used to belong to that guy Raffi."

"I loaned I.F.D. a box of old clothes for props. I got a feeling your shoes were in there." We walked through the workshop toward the big performance space. Mo wanted to check out the show, regardless. "It's like art where you could get hurt," he said.

"Mo, I can't do this."

"Ray."

"I'm not shitting you. I can't do it."

But Mo paid no attention, just led me into the hangar-sized space in which I.F.D. were about to do their thing. Floodlights lit a concrete floor on which the night's sacrificial idols awaited destruction: a pyramid of old televisions, a full-scale replica of, yet again, precisely the kind of stucco bungalow I'd grown up in, a cleverly done effigy of a popular Republican pundit, a Statue of Liberty, and, worst of all, a life-size mock-up of the Last Supper of Christ. With the Paul they were just adding, all twelve apostles stood in papier-mâché, and Christ even had his fingers dipped in a bowl of water.

"Mo," I said, "I can't watch this."

"Let me just find your shoes."

Looming around the doomed assemblages were the intended perpetrators, alarming scrap-metal robots with serious weaponry: a waist-high stainless-steel spider with a top-mounted flamethrower, a twelve-foot-tall machine with a tyrannosaurian jaw on front, and a tank that fired full beer cans from a rocket launcher.

"Mo, *please*," I said. "Just coming down to this place is enough for one day."

"Raymond, Raymond. Tell me more about this new girl while I figure out what they did with our stuff."

I wasn't in the mood. I should have been with her right then.

Above the growing audience, an oversized Hereford cow dangled from a girder. A sign on its neck read MAKE THE SWITCH TO ANGUS. Beneath it, in large fluorescent numbers, a millennial count-down clock started ticking toward 2000. A sharp whine started as a go-cart squirreled around with a goopy Jesus head completely enclosing its driver. A thruster-pipe looped over its back and glowed with jet heat as the cart skidded past: the show had begun. Mo was looking around pretty carefully, without luck. A concussion from a replica German missile engine bent the whole frame of the ware-house outwards, causing little windows to fall from the ceiling right into the crowd. That little spider scampered around now, too, belching fire as the bald guy ran along behind it with a radio control box.

I told Mo it looked like they planned to burn that Last Supper.

"That's kind of the beauty, though, huh?" Mo said. "If you think about it?"

I looked at him.

"I just mean it's nonreproduceable. The whole thing. It's kind of great to have something that's not a replica or a video or something, you know? Not even really a rehearsed performance that they could do again."

"Mo, what are you talking about?"

"It's like one of the last one-shot deals, and the fact you could die watching it—that's what pulls people out of their boringness and makes an epiphany for them. Their suburban experience gets remedied by *actual* experience. Think about that. *Having an actual experience.* It's practically outdated. So they make one for people and it freaks them out, because they forgot what it's like."

Another concussion shattered more little windows high overhead, sending still more glass tumbling down as that pyramid of old televisions began showing my favorite *Brady Bunch* episode—the one where Greg gets hurt surfing. Briefly, I found myself in the serenity of fourteen pyramidically arranged simulacra of my own childhood living room, Mom grading papers in the next room and both my sisters off playing somewhere. Then a plume of fire tore into the pyramid and those old vacuum tubes popped and Mom and the living room went up in smoke. A fifteen-foot tesla coil arced bolts of synthetic lightning through the building frame, almost as alive as the spidering fractures Mo and I had witnessed cracking High Sierra skies. The noise worsened, and I felt every rumble in my bones in a way I didn't like at all.

"Hey, Mo," I said loudly, to be heard. Suddenly, I needed to be absolutely sure. "Mo, you're going to tell your dad everything's okay, right?"

He just looked at me.

"Right? I mean, before we do the Captain, and all?"

"Ray . . ."

"I mean about this book I'm writing and all, that you're actually in. See, he wrote me . . ."

"I know, Ray." He wiped his hands on his jeans.

I caught my breath. "You okay with it?"

"That stuff's pretty personal for me."

"Personal?"

"Try to understand, huh?"

"What are you saying? I mean I just wanted to . . ."

"I'm just saying that stuff's pretty private."

"You're going to tell him, though, right? That it's okay?"

He looked around the big room. "It's not okay, Ray."

I stared at him.

"That whole thing with Lisa and the ptarmigan and everything. I was pretty bummed to read that."

Smoke billowed from floor pipes as a technician rushed out to help a failed machine that made a gang of dismembered, beheaded mannequins hump each other's ketchup-smeared neck stumps (horrifying, of course). Dumbfounded, I watched the artificial carnage and thought about weird things like what my daily drive to work would be like now that I'd finally have to give up writing and get a straight job and join the world. I imagined the hustling to pass or be passed in the Race of Life, with a little victory and failure every second, and how, when stuck in traffic, I'd roll down the window and accept suffering as a part of earthly life. And maybe it wouldn't be so bad. Maybe I'd look overhead at the office towers new and old and the blue sky above, and not mind being one of the well-adjusted grown-ups who worked all week for decent salaries at Masonite desks with loose-leaf calendars offering new obscure words for each day, complete with definitions and phonetic breakdowns, so you could walk into the lobby and ask the receptionist if she knew the meaning of *flib.ber.ti.gib.bet* (*n.* a chattering or flighty, light-headed person) and have her chuckle with traumatized embarrassment, or of *re.cru.desce* (*v.i.* to break out afresh, as a sore or a disease that has been quiescent; erupt), to which she'd just smile blankly.

"Can you understand?" Mo asked. "It's like, those stories weren't meant to be written down."

"Written down? Written down . . . yeah."

"It's not whether you wrote them, or somebody else, or even me. It's like I was just still telling them, you know? I wasn't even done with them yet, and it's like now I can't tell them. The way they end where you wrote them, that's how they end now, and I have to just live with that."

"You're going to let your dad do this."

"Ray, don't say it like that. It's just . . ."

"He called me a thief."

"I don't know what he called you, okay, and I

really, really do not want to talk about my father with you. I don't think you're a thief, anyway, it's just . . ."

"Just what?"

"I don't think anybody ever owns a story, okay? Either you or me." Mo paused.

"What are you trying to say?"

"It's just that writing ruins the telling, forever. That's all."

A robot walker with a spear lumbered toward that papier-mâché conservative pundit, who was now yelling at two mannequins with gashes in their breasts that sent fountains of blood arcing into each other's mouths. And then I saw them: my shoes. The Jesus mannequin had been dressed with my climbing shoes for the *faux* Last Supper. My perfectly worn-in, exquisitely sensitive Taos—the only pair of climbing shoes I felt absolutely comfortable in—were going to be incinerated.

"Hey, Ray," Mo said, "we got to do El Cap, huh? Without being too mad at each other? Ray, what are you doing?" Mo grabbed my arm as I climbed over the barricade.

"Just pretend, huh? Ray doesn't care too much about this, right? He'll get over it. He'll find something else to do." I don't know what was happening to me. I really don't. I just know that, at the time, nothing Mo'd said made any sense to me— it sounded like bullshit meant to beautify less noble emotions. The pundit's pants lay around his ankles and an AIDS Victim Identification Number graced his right butt-cheek. The pundit harangued from an internal tape recorder against the waste of federal funds on profane art while yellow fluid gushed from his garden-hose penis onto a Confederate flag. I remember telling Mo to let me get my goddamn climbing shoes so I'd never have to come down here or see him again, and I remember him holding on to my arm as that walker pulled to the pundit's rear, drew back its long, ashen lance, and thrust. Then it thrust again, thrashing through the layers of painted paper and tearing the pundit a new ass-hole, shaking the figure's frame until its pointing finger fell partly off. I swear I was just trying to jerk my arm free, but I guess my elbow caught Mo right in the eye.

Standing there alone, wanting to break something, I looked for one of the I.F.D. guys I knew. Tell him to go over to Jesus and get my climbing shoes. A robotic arm destroyed the countdown numbers like *T. rex*'s final bite at a pterodactyl during the dinosaurian holocaust. Only the Last Supper remained standing, and that flamethrowing spider flickered with sparks as its limbs jerked to life. It began to take aim. Fucking Mo. I don't know what came over me, but when that pincer arm had finally destroyed the clock at a few moments before the year 2000, and a coarse, electric buzz had grown louder from the swinging cow, I did something absolutely uncharacteristic. I walked right out in front of everybody,

marched toward that banquet table and all those
sloppy, pastel apostles—Peter, Paul, and Andrew,
the two Jameses and John, Philip and Bartholomew, Thomas and Matthew, Simon the Canaanite,
and, of course, Judas Iscariot laughing out loud.

The flame hit the two Jameses first. Their heads
evaporated, and then their crepe-paper gowns vanished in curly poofs. Simon went the same way, and
then Bartholomew. I was worried about getting
burned, but when the flamethrower was halfway to
Jesus, who had one hand in a dish of water and the
other held up in benediction, I couldn't take it. I
couldn't lose Raffi's old Taos. The bald I.F.D. tech
guy started yelling at me to get the hell out of the
way, and the audience booed, but I wasn't having
any. The second James collapsed in ashes as I bent
over and tried to untie my shoes from Jesus' feet,
but the flamethrower tore through John before I
could free even one. Christ was next, so I stood up,
wrapped my arms around Jesus from behind, and
tried to drag Him out of the line of fire. Jesus
weighed a lot more than I expected, and I really
had to wrap both arms around Him and kind of
waddle backwards. I would have made it, too, but
the flames from Judas licked at Jesus' paper clothes
until flames spread down His legs. I had to let go,
and I took off my T-shirt to smother the flames on
Jesus' feet, hoping to save my climbing shoes. I
guess those assholes didn't have any way to stop
the flamethrower midperformance, and I probably
would've been killed if it hadn't been for that cow
overhead, which had been dripping white fluid for

several minutes. I was looking around for a hose or anything to douse Jesus' legs, but then the cow's midsection convulsed once as if about to give birth. With a sharp, bright bang, its leather and vinyl skin ruptured like an overfilled football, and the payload—hundreds of gallons of rank, spoiled cream and rotten eggs—blew the sculpture apart and cascaded onto a half-charred Jesus and myself.

When I finally got up, Mo was nowhere to be seen. Most of the crowd had been cleared out by several policemen—apparently I.F.D. hadn't gotten a permit for all the explosives. I pulled my scorched climbing shoes off the smoldering wreckage. The beautifully stitched leather uppers were okay, but the rubber soles—the essential ingredients—had both melted and peeled halfway off. I walked around awhile, dumbfounded. Wiped curdled milk out of my ears and eyes and tried to find Mo. No luck, though. Not even back at his school bus among those creepy storage pens. I waited around for half an hour, and eventually got cold with my clothes all wet. The truck was still parked there, full of all the gear. So I drove it down to that roll-up door and let myself out of the building. On the street again, I saw what could've been Mo, riding his motorcycle past a yard full of rusted yellow tractors. But when I sped after the figure, it had disappeared.

Midway on my Saturday's journey, among waving hills of grassy tectonic ripple, the pagodalike Chinese Camp schoolhouse baked in the Indian summer sun. I didn't feel like driving all the way up Evan's private dirt road, so I turned the truck's engine off and got out to call. A few sitting women and drunks lingered behind the village's shutters in the remote heat, waiting. A small farmhouse advertised the Kiwi Tavern, Chinese Camp general store, and Chinese Camp post office. After that long drive alone, I felt a little fuzzy from a combination of intense inwardness and wide-open gazing. I'd brooded clear across the Bay Bridge to Oakland, through the coastal range, and down to the flat burning heat of the Central

Valley—there to face gleaming malls and Masonite tract homes festering across California's interior plains like an undiagnosed malignancy. At least after Manteca, agriculture did still reign: late-harvest tomato trucks had been running the survey-line highways and the dusty roadside fruit stands were nearing the end of their season. Then I really started to relax as the road climbed into the Sierra foothills.

Feeling pretty stupid about my little fight with Mo, I'd spent much of the prior night driving around looking for the guy. I'd checked his favorite dive bars, a childhood friend's place in Diamond Heights, even his ex-girlfriend's place in the Richmond. I hadn't found him, and, after sleeping awhile at home, I'd returned to the warehouse to find Mo's bus all padlocked. The bald I.F.D. guy, drinking orange juice in the show's carnage, had seen Mo take off on a motorcycle. I sat around awhile, trying to guess where he'd gone and what the big deal was. Finally, I decided he'd probably headed up to Yosemite alone, knowing I'd follow with all the gear. So I bought coffee and a muffin at a corner market and set out after him. Hoping Evan would keep me company while I looked for Mo at the river, I parked the truck now at Chinese Camp. I took off my sweater and jeans, pulled on shorts, stepped over to the pay phone, and told Evan to beat it on down to the Kiwi Tavern. Then I decided to buy myself a mint ice-cream sandwich dipped in chocolate. Ice cream could have been a little hard to stomach so soon after that cow fiasco, but Mo and I had always felt you had to eat ice cream out there in the foothills. It had to do with the heat and the culture.

A Ford Mustang convertible sat in front of the tavern with its top down. An enormous, Scooby-doo-like spike-collared dog sat chained in the back seat. The size of a small horse, that dog made me nervous as hell. I gave the Mustang a wide berth, and stepped onto the porch, then inside. A taxidermed stag's head hung next to a dusty bear's over the gaunt woman proprietor and her only customer at the backroom bar: a shirtless, goateed, and tattooed live-wire of a human who doubtless owned that Mustang. Canned and packaged food cluttered the unlit aisles, and beer trays hung on the walls. Racks of porn gathered dust by the old-fashioned brass register: *Barely Legal* had a feature story on how "Cover Girl Nitzie Fingers Her Nude Nookie," *Black Tail* had "Summer Clam Fest '94," and *Shaved Sexy Action* had a news flash on how "Eddy Sticks His Tongue Straight into Gina's Creamy Crack!" When considered together with the chewing gum, kids' breakfast cereals, and 30/ .06 rifle ammunition, the whole made just enough cultural clutter for that quiet interior to feel like an actual place, a sufficiently complete reality to compete with the not-quite-tamed foothills outside. I don't mean there were grizzlies playing salmon handball or wolves flaying fauns downriver. It's just that those surrounding hills of golden grass were so spare and soft, so easily bulldozed, that in all those years up here with Mo I'd never stopped thinking they had nothing to do with America, were more fit for soft-stepping quiet people with small appetites and immediate gods.

I bought that ice cream and stepped back outside. From a shady bench in the blistering dust, I ignored that monstrous hound and looked up toward the world of the river and Mo and white granite. A single black raven shone inky on a power line, a spot of tar blurring in the sky. The oily smell of the road overwhelmed the wheaty reek of dead grass, and both the high mountain eastern skies and the western coastal range hung brown in the pale blue, each blurred by its own brand of combustion: one by city smog; the other by country wildfire. Late-summer California was choked and sickly, ready for the cleansing rains of winter. As I sucked at my dripping ice cream and waited for Evan, I took in the crickets, pricklers, and rattlesnakes on baked soil, heard the quivering stillness of barbed oak leaves, and held my breath to test my new intuition that my whole life up to that instant had been just that—an instant. I got this feeling that being on the road, and even sitting on that bench, *mattered*, that it was exactly what I was supposed to do.

I saw a CalTrans worker in an orange shirt contemplate a small pile of tarred gravel he'd apparently been assigned to remove from the roadway. He took off his orange hard hat, wiped his brow, and looked over to me with a smile I couldn't decode. When he pulled a shovel out of his orange truck, I stepped back inside the store to use the men's room. I was sent across a little "Biergarten" with a single threadbare Cinzano umbrella stabbed into the sun-slain grass. In a white outhouse, a "donations" jar collected tourist money like rainwater. No crippling choice between Sure and Unsure, and there was something serene about that bright room and its chromed mirror, the mothbally smell of the urinal disinfectant and the uncomplicated life implied by the unfinished floor planks. The bright light in there and the piss on the floor did make me wonder why the hell I couldn't just be happy with a small dream, a possible dream. Like maybe get an adobe shack with Fiona down in Todos Santos. She could sell good art to hip tourists, and we'd drink margaritas outside the local Hotel California and call it a day. Stop worrying so much.

When I returned to the wheat and tar, Evan still not there, mirage puddles shimmered on the sun-softened roadway. The guy with the shovel had given up, sat reading the Oakdale paper in his air-conditioned truck—motor running, smelly exhaust making a little waving warp of heat blur. No anxiety, no hypertension, no visible self-loathing. I sat back down on that shiny-smooth ass-worn bench, leaned against a window plastered with cartoon breasts selling cigarettes, and opened another ice-cream sandwich—vanilla this time, no complaints. Heat waved up off ancient cattle ranches with air-conditioned ranch homes full of home electronics and jumbo freezers that kept entire dismembered cows ice-cold in the 110-degree heat. Soon, an orange CalTrans shovel tractor crawled along the shoulder, kicking up dust as its driver sipped a sixty-four-ounce soda. He stopped next to the tiny pile of offending gravel, looked down at it, looked at the first guy, and chuckled. Big project for a hot day, but somehow these guys calmly inhabited their lives. Which was bullshit, but smart. Deep. A distinct sign of maturity. Of saying, Hey now, this is it. Show up every morning, sniff some tar, and do it—take a few steps, manifest a livable life without regrets. The tractor didn't have any luck with the little pile, either. It had solidified in the sun and refused to be shoveled. So, when a huge orange dump truck drove in from the east, they still didn't have a payload. The newcomer killed his engine and got out to chat. The first guy smiled that enviable smile again, and I decided it revealed a bemused disbelief at his destiny—a yielding to his temporary role as butt of the cosmic joke, and a sense of comfort in the knowledge that we *all* were in our own private ways.

Evan's black BMW crunched across the gravel and he parked next to that Mustang. He hopped out and slammed the door, then took off his aviator sunglasses and gave me his bizarre shit-eating grin. I've never known what a shit-eating grin is really supposed to be, but if anybody's got one, it's little Evan. He knew better than to ask why I was alone, so we just smiled at each other and stepped back into the cool tavern to forage for enough sweat-box chili dogs, Spicy Ranchero potato chips, shrink-wrapped barbecued chicken, Mystic Mint cookies, Coca-Cola, and Snickers bars to feed three.

We were assuming we'd find Mo. While Evan paid, I returned to the heat out front, and found Scooby-doo sitting upright in the Mustang's front seat. I knew how the canine mind worked—pure intimidation—so I stared back, steeled my jaw, started a low growl, and watched those vacant orbs weigh my soul's willingness to die.

"Did you know redheads are statistically stingier than other people?" Evan asked, appearing beside me with a paper bag.

The beast lunged toward me in outrage, hitting the end of its chain so hard it nearly tore out the car's steering column. I dumped Coke all over my bare chest as it pawed against the already shredded upholstery, muscles rippling beneath its taut skin and those curved wet teeth more than adequate to slaughter me. Then the tavern door opened again and that live-wire human ran barking back up to the rabid nightmare creature with an exuberant smile, saying, "Sick 'em, Psycho! Tear their *fucking* throats out! Yeah, boy, niggers with guns! Niggers with *fucking* Uzis! Oooh, that's a good boy, give Daddy a kiss."

Evan had had a wonderful night at the cabin, he told me as we drove off, leaving my truck at the tavern. He'd stayed up late on the deck, soaking in the nighttime heat, doing bong hits, and listening over and over to an acoustic Grateful Dead bootleg from Harper's College. Now, on the highway toward the river, he loaded, rolled, licked, and lit a joint while cackling with mad glee, mimicking that freak in the store: "Niggers with Uzis! Ah ha! Downright *Deliverance*-style crackers out here, Raymond! The pointy-eared, webbed-toed unconscious speaks! *Squeal* like a pig, motherfucker!"

When he tuned into my dour mood, Evan asked if I'd had fun with Fiona.

"I had a great time," I said.

"Details, man. Details."

"Well, she told me an amazing story about her mom dying."

"Her mom died recently?"

"Last month."

"Ouch."

"No kidding."

"The mystery solved, huh? Of why she's out here?"

"I guess so."

I told Evan about Mo's dad's letter then.

"You really write some of Mo's stories?" Evan asked.

"Evan."

"Well, did you? You never told me that."

"Who wouldn't? They're great stories."

"Yeah, I guess Mr. Lehrman's being harsh, huh?"

"Harsh? It's unbelievable."

"You talk to Mo yet?"

I said I had.

"You get in a fight or something?"

"Last night."

"I thought you went out with Fiona last night."

"After dinner."

Evan paused to think. "Wait a minute," he said. "She tells you about her mom dying and you just split?"

I nodded.

"Raymond, what the hell are we going to do with you?"

I was even going to miss her gallery opening. In

fact, if I was lucky enough to find Mo, I wouldn't see her for a week or two. I fell silent and watched the forest, thought how the million individual moments going by outside were all moments one could know well—another leaf flipping in the breeze or a lightning-stricken pine finally falling to the ground, all of it smeared into "forest" by the pressure that eighty m.p.h. puts on your ability to make sense of the world. Along the Gold Rush highway, through timber and mining country, the radio announced rapidly spreading forest fires at higher elevation, even a threat that they might have to close Yosemite National Park.

"Dope-ijuana?" Evan asked.

"Nope. I quit."

It was so hot that Evan's leather seats were sweating, and without warning he electronically rolled up all the windows and the sunroof. "Don't get so wrapped up in this, Ray."

I asked what he meant.

"I don't know, just . . . You remember that time I saw Mo on 16th Street? In front of Dalva, standing there drunk off his ass?"

I didn't.

"I'm just saying Mo's got a lot going on that's not about you. He was talking to this homeless guy under the Roxie marquee, calling him 'Mo' and asking how he ended up on the streets. I'm standing there watching, and Mo passes out flat on his face. I mean *flat*. Like I actually heard the sound of his forehead hitting the sidewalk. It made me sick. You don't remember this? I had to call 911, and the paramedics said Mo'd taken too much aspirin and it thinned out his blood, so a little alcohol took him out."

"Evan," I asked, "are you trying to secondhand smoke me out?"

"Ever since my bride made me quit," Evan said, turning the heat on, "I've been enjoying a little weed now and then *so* much."

"Why are you turning on the heater?"

"Well, it's just too damn hot out, isn't it?"

"You going to put on the AC?"

"It's broken." He flipped the heat up to full and in minutes I dripped from every pore and my thighs stuck to the seat. Evan had done some auto-lock antichild thing, so I couldn't get my window back down. Still sucking hard at his joint, Evan reveled in my misery and filled the car with smoke.

"I'm going to lose my license," Evan grumbled, eyes on the rearview mirror: no more than a few miles from the river, and a Highway Patrol car was directly behind us. Evan gnashed his teeth as he pulled over, rolled down all the windows, cranked up the fans, and shoved the contraband under his seat. Ninety-degree air poured in. "Beautifully cool, huh?" Evan said. "Don't you feel great now? By comparison?"

"Son," the handsome young officer said, "you know, there was a forty-five sign back there, I don't know if . . ."

"Where?" Evan snapped—aviator sunglasses still on—as if the cop had made the whole thing up just to be spiteful.

"Well, back around the corner. A lot of people miss it, so I . . ."

"That's bullshit," Evan growled, craning his unusually long neck out the window to look. "There's *no* sign back there."

The officer stepped back. "Well," he said, "it's new. A lot of people who drive this road frequently haven't gotten used to it, so if you . . ."

"Well I drive this road *all* the time. And I have *not* seen any sign there. You can't expect me to . . ."

"Give me your license and registration."

Evan cursed that cop for miles, and nearly took us head-on into the first of ten identical caravaning green RVs with Canadian license plates. When the danger had passed, I took to watching a Southern Pacific train of chemical tank cars and empty boxcars rumble along a willow-shadowed river. For a while we ran even with it, and I saw a woman and man sitting in an empty boxcar. Where the tracks veered away from the highway, along a river, we turned off toward the swimming hole. No Mo motorcycle visible right off, but we decided to look anyway. Walked along a blackberry-brambled footpath to where granite slabs walled in a clear pool in the middle of the river. A cable ran between trees on either side of the stream, and a tribe of naked hippies sunbathed on a rock while a few rednecks splashed about in their Levi's. Evan didn't like the naked longhair leather-anklets and unfiltered-apple-juice scene, and Mo wasn't around, so we headed upriver, toward the more secluded hole Mo and I had always used.

The trail wound along a path that dipped into a grove of oaks with little campsites and bark carvings, even a shrine of sacred vegetables stacked next to a cracked geode that bristled with purple crystals. A ratty bedroll lay in the shade. Soon, there were few overt signs of people, and we wandered for half an hour along slippery rocks, falling into the icy water, then splashing back onto the trail to get covered with dust. Tore skin here and there on little branches and, though a faint yellow haze had come across the sky, began burning in the open sun. Feeling my bare feet once again on the smooth solidity of white Sierra granite, and slipping my fingers in boulder cracks, I copped again that incomparable feeling of flesh upon the world's raw material. I stepped carefully from rock to rock and tried to find the center of my balance again, to get quiet enough inside to move gracefully and steadily. Eventually, Evan and I did come to the pool where swirling snowmelt had eroded a midstream boulder into an elegantly rounded likeness of a cetacean, but Mo wasn't there either.

Evan took out his little bag of buds and lit up a small waterpipe. "Dope-ijuana?" he asked again.

"I've already lost too much of myself."

"Nah, bullshit. Loosen up. I'm getting married forever."

The stream flushed clear and bright across our toes. "Herbology?" I asked. All suffering comes from desire. No roses in cardboard sheaths carried across mountain ranges.

"Yep, shmerbalism." Evan packed a bud into the bowl with his butt in a little dish of stone, toes in the icy water.

Sure, or Unsure. "Just burn it?"

"What? Yeah." He handed me his lighter.

"Just suckle, burn, and breathe?" I asked.

"You're doing that Mo-talk thing. Cut that out."

When I handed the pipe back, Evan got the whole chamber full of smoke, capped it, took a breather, then sucked down the cloud in one athletic gasp. He sank deep into the water, hesitated for a moment six feet under, gave a full-body dolphin kick and vanished under the whale-shaped rock. A minute later he surfaced coughing smoke on the far side of the creek—with a real job and getting married and even a jointly owned dog. Evan had just manifested a life and decided to be happy with it, as if he'd checked out somehow and declared his life's story complete. It made me feel like I'd been sprinting through the train station of life, running alongside the Pullman car holding all my best friends when, just at the moment of grasping the handrail, I'd run right off the end of the platform.

"I mean," I said across the river, referring to my own life, "no choices consciously made, no pattern seen, or maybe I'm just reading order back into what's really an inchoate set of experiences for you, too, Evan."

"What are you talking about?"

"It's like life's this geologic flow, like a mountain range that's lifting or a coast that's rising, you know? Too slow to see the pattern so you need one of those cameras where they speed up the blooming of a rose? But on your life."

"Opie, relax."

"You're just so successful, Evan. You've got your life. Just doing your job, making money, not complaining." The creek steadily drained High Sierra meadows, ran snowmelt through us, around us, down toward the sea. A late-summer furnace of soil and stone, that canyon heated by the hour. "Even right now," I said, "I could be a Navy SEAL, like this friend of mine who plants limpet mines on the bottoms of destroyers and gets shot out of the torpedo tubes of submarines in full scuba gear. He was actually called up early for the Panama invasion, where all those SEALs died. He got ashore, walked up to some guard post, aimed, pulled the trigger, and watched this Panamanian guy's head spray all over a wall. You know what he did? He turned around, went back to the ship, and quit. So I guess that doesn't sound like something I'd want to do. But at least it was *something*. I mean, you, too. We're both the right age, pretty athletic. We could easily just show up and declare ourselves professionals and patriots. Nobody's stopping us."

Evan stood on a white slab that bordered one side of the pool, daring the forest to confront his nakedness the way he'd often dared whole cocktail parties. "You know what the SEALs do on your birthday?" Evan asked. "They strip you naked, tie you up with duct tape, and lash you to a running cold shower so they can shave your pubic hair and eyebrows and whip you with wet towels." He held a Frisbee and motioned for me to climb a rock to receive it.

"I just meant I *could* be one. At least in theory. I could be anything. But you're right. You're right."

Evan grumbled that he honestly had no idea what the hell I was talking about. I guessed I didn't either. The water was bitter cold, and its flow was low and sluggish this late in a hot summer that seemed to be lasting well into autumn. A big black bird soared the thermal over the river canyon, above piñon pines and manzanita, looking for the weak and diseased of the forest's floor dwellers. Coasting, hunting, just doing it—at one.

"See that vulture?" I said, next to Evan again. "I love vultures."

Evan had given up on the Frisbee, lay spread out on a hot slab. I joined him there, baked between sun above and the deep heat of fired granite, imagined myself an expired desert corpse awaiting the buzzard-belly express train to physio-spiritual return. Only a faint stirring midstream marked the current. Trout behind stones. One could, potentially, have taken a deep-enough breath to keep floating belly-up, to ripple and slide around all those snow-white granite tumbledown boulders, meander across deep-green trout pools, and wash clear out of the mountains into the dead fisheries of the San Joaquin River, among the delta's grassy islands and eventually into the broad currents of the San Francisco Bay shipping lanes, under the Golden Gate Bridge and out with the tidal plume to the open, empty, sharky Pacific.

Back where we'd parked, I noticed a familiar yellow VW microbus resting in the shade. A graphic of Buddha floated over a blue sunset on the side, a mountain bike hung on a rear rack, and a big-wall haul bag sat outside. One of many bumper stickers read "Wall Drug." While Evan unlocked his car, I wandered over to have a closer look. Mounted along one side of the van was a big sheet of plywood full of finger-sized holes for dangling by the hour and strengthening your digits. On a nearby log, a decent-looking redheaded kid was telling a wraith-like girl how they should form a human assembly line to roll vegan burritos for tonight's show.

"Betchew they'll play a Shakedown," the girl

said back, irrelevantly. "Last night I heard they did a Scarlet-Fire right into Estimated-Eyes and then teased Saint Stephen during Space, but they ended up playing Shakedown. I'm *dying* for a Shake-down."

Such parched, barren heat there in the hills. "Fire on the Mountain" played on the van's tape deck, and climbing hardware lay all over a picnic table. A shirtless man and a very tanned Asian woman in a blue shirt sorted through the gear, putting little daubs of blue and yellow paint on each, and mumbling, *"Hare, hare, hare ganja."* Then the guy stopped sorting gear and looked aimlessly at his truck. "I think it's time for a change," he said. "Too many Dead stickers. It's time to make it more the sort of general peace-slash-climbing machine. More sort of Save the Humans; Love Your Mother; Earth is a Beautiful Place, or So It Looks from Space. Maybe keep 'Chouinard Equipment for Al-pinists' and 'Space Is for Deadheads, Not War-heads.'" He appeared to have no body fat at all. His ribs showed below flagstone pectoral muscles, and his deltoids were like wings. His forearms had a disturbing number of veins, like electrical wires carrying a dangerous excess of current.

Then he turned toward me, and I realized I knew that chiseled, scar-covered face: it was Yabber, the very guy who'd sent Mo and me to Yosemite and sold us all those magic mushrooms once we got there. Back when Mo and I first moved to Yosem-ite, Yabber won $5,000 in the NBC Survival of the Fittest, a race where you do an open-water swim, run up hills carrying five-gallon pails of water, and cross an obstacle course. The win had gotten him so excited, he'd spent the whole $5,000 on an Italian racing bike and decided he was going to be a professional triathlete. In our tent one night, after Mo and I had had a pretty hair-raising mushroom experience on top of Half Dome (causing me to forever swear off psycho-actives on the grounds that my unconscious was too unstable for reckless unpacking), we'd heard crashing in the campground. I'd looked out and seen Yabber—whose girlfriend had apparently just broken up with him—smashing that new bike back and forth against a picnic table. He'd lifted the bike over his head and wrapped it around an outdoor barbecue. Then he'd walked past our tent and, in a perfectly friendly voice, said, "Hey, dudes."

I didn't think Yabber recognized me, but I was completely wrong. He thrust out a powerful hand and grinned all over, offered me a piece of wheat bread and some cheese. He seemed genuinely excited to see me, and he told those Deadheads that my buddy Mo and I were legitimate hard-core Valley rats, which wasn't really true. When I asked, Yabber claimed to have seen Mo just that morning. He even thought Mo was going to the show that night. Evan lit up at the prospect of following Mo there, but I was worried about getting sidetracked by hearsay.

"Come on," Evan said, "let's go acid-dance with big-titted hippy chicks."

"And," Yabber added, "seeing as to how we're all friends here, and you boys are on a bit of a mission, how about Yabs sets you up like old times?" He handed a blue plastic baggie to Evan. It was full of dry blue-stemmed mushrooms. Yabber loved playing the guru dispensing amulets of power. "That Mo guy's radical, by the way," Yabber said. "He was telling me about riding a beach cruiser clear to Baja with his longboard. You hear about this?"

I nodded.

"I love that guy. He's just like his old man. He's going up on the Big Stone again, too."

"Did he say that?"

"Yep."

I asked who he was doing it with, and Yabber surprised me by pausing to think. He surprised me even more by confessing he didn't know—that he'd seen Mo hanging at the river with some long-hair climbers, and thought he might be doing it with them. I couldn't believe it.

Now I really had to catch up with Mo. "Yabber," I said, "you know Raffi pretty well, right?"

"Jesus of Camp Four?"

"He still fixing shoes?"

"I guess. I don't know. I'm the wrong guy to ask, really. I got a little too under his spell."

I remembered then that Yabber'd just done his sixtieth ascent of El Capitan, this time alone. There's a way you can belay yourself while climbing, anchoring the rope below while you ascend, then above while you bring up your gear. It requires doing the entire wall three times. "What's it really like up on El Cap, anyway?" I asked. "When you get higher up?"

Four yellow fire trucks rumbled over the creek's bridge as Yabber told me he'd gotten hammered by weather up there just this spring. In his jittery, almost feminine voice, he said his van had been out of commission and he'd split up with yet another chick, so he'd hitchhiked to the Valley, borrowed gear from one of his Search and Rescue buddies, and started up alone. Nine days, it took. Yabber talked with a vague self-mockery, an irony about it all.

The heat grew with the day, and sparrows played in the oaks around our heads. "But what was it *like*?" I asked, perhaps imagining he could answer the question I hadn't yet named. "Just being up there, I mean?"

"Great. I'd roust in the morning on a ledge," Yabber said, "crawl out of my bag for tea, listen to some speed metal at max volume, and suck a few bong loads with my Advil to ease the pain." Yabber'd also seen a BASE jumper leap off the Captain. Saw him all the way down, and his parachute never opened at all. Yabber'd been standing on a little stopper in a thin crack, and heard the guy hooting, and then something broke and the guy picked up speed and kept going faster and faster until he screamed, Look out below! "The guy skipped off a slab at the base," Yabber told me, "and just disintegrated."

This made me a little faint.

Yabber said he'd gotten to a ledge, drunk three King Cobra tall boys, and toasted the Big Stone God. And then it had started to rain. As Yabber began talking about the storm, I looked up to the jagged patch of sky visible through the treetops, saw several big prop planes pass over, off to water-bomb the fire. "Five days on one ledge," Yabber said, "with these updrafts slapping me around, but you know what? I had my ghetto blaster cranking in my little bivy sack, and I kept playing this video football game and thinking, Jesus, if my mom only knew how fucking weird I am." He laughed out loud at the thought, delighted and bewildered by himself.

My palms were very damp now with fear, but I absolutely had to know what had happened.

"I know what you're asking," Yabber said. "You should probably look Raffi up one of these days. That's his department. All I know is that the last twenty-four hours was like this horrid nightmare I was stuck in. I'd wake up 'cause my body temperature was dropping, shaking all over, and what totally saved my ass was these Jolly Rancher candies. If someone had said, 'Would you sell your soul for some more Jolly Ranchers?' I would have done it. I could've radioed for a rescue, but I saw the window to the next stage, where the easiest way out is to say goodbye. I saw that door and chose to go through it." He paused to stretch in the sun.

"Yeah, and?" I demanded, my face flushed.

"Even when I thought I was dying, I said okay. But then I woke up again, like, 'Hm, I'm not dead.' That point, that's what you're trying to achieve, and afterwards, I was like, 'Wow, that was fucking rad.' And a week later I was doing it again."

The little highway slowed through a Gold Rush town where death by hanging was to the local culture what the Declaration of Independence is to Philadelphia. A brick hotel offered sightseers a Victorian prostitute hanging in effigy from a hangman's block, not swinging at all in the still foothills air. Her neck gave no appearance of having broken in the initial fall or elongated in the implied hundred years since her sentence was carried out by the county Junior League. Onwards, the road wound among bewitchingly soft crests and troughs of bronzed wild wheat and modest mobile homes as the sun slid toward the distant coastal mountains. Most of the Digger pine, blue oak, and buckeyes crowded together around streams and ponds, but a few big valley oaks had their own hillocks. Hundreds of miles of sky congealed into a band of luminescent purple, and a few far-off cities clustered their twinkling glow in the vast inkwell of the Central Valley. Nearing the fairground, we saw more and more junky old cars full of longhairs en route to the show, and we exchanged knowing grins with them as Evan passed in third gear.

We parked in a dusty lot teeming with humans selling food and jewelry. No sign of Mo, but plenty of stinky, goofball kids playing out their little bliss fantasies. A wispy teenage girl in a loose skirt wandered by selling vegan cookies, saying some horseshit like, "Don't got cash, how about a song? Just put a smile on my face . . ." A Hindu woman with bookishly sexy eyes and bare feet wove past holding up a finger and carrying a cardboard sign that read "I Need a Miracle—Just One." Such modest demands! (And the Lord said unto her, What *is* that in thine hand? And she said, It is a sign. And the Lord said, Cast it on the ground. And she cast it on the ground, and it became a Dead ticket; and she fled before it. And the Lord said unto her, Put forth thine hand, and take it by the stub. And she put forth her hand and took it by the stub, and caught it, and went into the show among her sisters and brothers, That they may believe that the Lord God of their heroes, the God of Jerry and Bobby, hath appeared unto her.)

I've told about the fear of chaos that so plagued me back then, so you won't be surprised to learn that I'd had a conflicted relationship with hallucinogens since the night in tenth grade when mushrooms had led me to taste every single substance in Mo's family kitchen. His father had found me naked on the linoleum, wallowing in a witch's brew of Grape-Nuts, vodka, and Ajax, and had sent me home exposed and humiliated. Then there'd been all those lost weeks in Yosemite with Mo, feeling the heron's hunger and the jackal's rending claw: profoundly fulfilling in the moment, deeply unsatisfying soon after. And, finally, there'd been that encounter with absolute anomie at the brink of Half Dome, that spiraling sense of the permanent incoherence of self. But, like a fool, I now joined Evan in blithely slathering those blue-streaked stems with almond butter and gobbling. Sucked some orange soda, and gobbled more. After half an hour, no pixels flashed along the rims of my vision and no colors trailed behind moving objects. In short, no tripping. I should've been glad, just eaten a tofu dog and relaxed, or remembered how long it takes that stuff to digest. But there's something very sad about eating hallucinogens and not tripping. It's like you finally admitted you believed in magic only to find it a big lie. So I ate a bunch more. Waited for Evan to brush his teeth (which he did at least four times a day, maybe more), and thought how the crowd certainly seemed happy enough and friendly enough, even if I didn't see Mo. Then we wound with the hordes toward fairground gates decorated in rose-crowned skeletons and skulls with lightning bolts in their brains. I had a vague apprehension as we neared the laughing death masks, but also felt it was time I went along for a ride, any ride. Then we paid and slipped inside. The music started and Evan put his arm around me and handed me a tofu dog and a beer, encouraging me to join this sweet, pointless club of connectedness. Just as I started eating, that woman from Yabber's van gazed into me with bloodshot wise-woman eyes. She now wore a sundress in the same yellow as Fiona's favorite T-shirt, and her face said she knew very well the journey I'd begun.

Then she looked away and the edges of my vision shimmered, then stopped, then shimmered again as if the snorkeling mask of tolerable comprehension had suddenly started to leak water. Odd, knowing a giant program was irrevocably jacked in to your metabolism, that little reactions were starting even as personality itself began to feel no more nor less than a mere patterned string of little reactions. Evan looked at me through the crowd with wide eyes and I shot up through a plane of light, and then another, and then every boogying hair-farmer at last began to streak light. Oak trees outside the fairground etched out blazing fields of sunset color and evening darkness. Sliding off the sweat-slippery arms of others, worrying I'd miss Mo if things got too weird, I ducked the flailing arms of a biker hate monster and, during a melodic lull, found myself among deeply concerned bootleg tapers. Gaunt-faced, with tight ponytails and fanny-packs full of audio equipment, they stood in a staked-out cluster before the sound boards. Their microphones reached like periscopes out of the crowd to catch the pure Word of the Boys—which at that moment was a silly lullaby about "We can share the women, we can share the wine."

Away from those grave apostles and shaking Quakers, I found myself sitting in the dirt among a squadron of tie-dyed quadriplegics. Their scraggly, bearded heads with blissfully lidless eyes bounced ecstatically atop their motorized chairs. Then that woman appeared and shook me and said I'd better get up. I rolled out of the way just as a red-eyed teenager opened his braces-ridden mouth to spew malt liquor and Canadian-bacon pizza right where I'd been sitting. Mortified, I found a gap under the fence and crawled through, clawed across dirt, and vomited myself, as if I'd been waiting months to vomit on an open hillside of grass and oak. Then I took long strides across crackling dry grain like I'd ridden ponies through at summer camp. The western horizon shone with moon-dusk, and sweeps of creamy stars brightened the mountain sky. A single jet plane blinked its red way across the States, trapped in its cherished illusion that acceleration might contract time and space into a manageable volume. I heard the boys singing "Ashes, ashes, all fall down," and thought, *Right on! I get it! I do! It's all about being grateful to have passed through the film between life and death and to be freed from wanting things you can't name much less have!* A blunt-headed barn owl melted out of a high branch and loped through the deep-blue night. I figured Mo'd find me out there by default—that we'd talk things over and be reasonable and be friends again, and that he'd tell his dad everything was cool, and then everything would be cool.

Evan, at the fence, asked what the hell I was doing. A thin, petulant voice from far away, he wanted to know if I'd found Mo yet, or what? I told him I was pretty sure Mo was out here, but Evan just disappeared into the crowd again. I decided I needed to escape the music still more, and reduce the number of voices in my head. So I drifted away in a cool breeze, waved off two mosquitoes, stumbled in gopher holes, and picked up seeds in my socks and hair and clothes, and then it happened. The boundaries of my being blurred the way they did with that staggeringly lovely young woman who'd hiked with me and punched me and then made love with me, who'd even spoken her most up-to-the-minute truths to me. I even thought of going to church with Fiona, as if I were at once utterly helpless and perfectly safe in this great sphere guarded over by my membership in the night. Loving the gift Yabber had given me, I felt the anxiety of self-consciousness wash off. I lay down under the stars finally free of human silliness, weighed a thousand pounds pressing against the hot earth like that trillion-pound El Capitan somewhere up in the cooler mountain air. The smokey-red eastern mountain horizon bubbled away and golden stalks of wild dry grain tickled my face for hours and hours. A nearby oak gave just the slightest billowing frame to an ocean of blue darkness—oneness, for once: a long, slowing time of thrilled-to-goofiness joy at the quiet, cricket-echoing night just happening absently onwards as my back and kidneys and lungs throbbed against the soil at a thousand gravities and I thought, *Yes, yes, yes . . . I'm feeling that feeling at last . . .*

"Did you know you're lying in cow shit?"

"No," I said to Evan, happily imagining that shit could no longer touch me and wanting to draw even the sickly looking Evan down into my arms. "I mean, yes, I *do* know, but it's not like that . . ." The drum improv began, and smiling heads moseyed around in the half-glow. Evan had done some uppers that weren't so up, and as he bent over to vomit beside me in the grass, I could see his spine jutting up through his filthy T-shirt. He fell to his knees, bloodying them as his nose drained into the puddle of his half-digested death-fungi, barbecued chicken, and ranch-flavored tortilla chips. Which did little for my sense of Connectedness to All Things. But then I saw a six-foot knob-head bobbing around.

"Evan," I said, "there he is! There's fucking Mo!"

"Well, go grab him," Evan grumbled, wiping his mouth with his T-shirt.

I pushed through the crowd toward Mo, and got everything ready I wanted to say—mostly just a bunch of self-serving baloney about how all I'd wanted was to let everyone know what a hero Mo was, and what a great storyteller, and how his dad had just wanted to get us apart. I wouldn't say that last part, of course, because you can't say bad things about a guy's dad. But I did want to tell Mo he'd always been right about my not taking enough risks, and that he also had to stop running away and beware of the nightmare right around life's corner, trouble behind the next tree, and to realize these were *dreams* he'd been trafficking in, and that you always either woke up from dreams or drowned in their rivers.

"Hey, Mo!" I yelled, as I got close.

I touched him on the shoulder and he spun around.

"What?" he asked.

"Nothing."

"What?" The guy just flat out, unequivocally, was not Mo Lehrman.

"I thought you were someone else." Which left me walking pretty aimlessly through the crowd, sick of the pursuit and sick of the whole story, and wanting to just go home and give up. When I found Evan again, I told him what had happened. Figured it was time to forget about the wall and let life drift on to tropical languor and love like it ought to have done ages ago. Call Fiona, apologize for leaving early last night, and see what she was doing right, exactly, then. Except that I knew what she was doing right then. Or—I looked at my watch—what she *had* been doing a few hours ago. I slipped past the food booths and First Aid tent to a row of pay phones, waited patiently for a weeping man to hang up. Tore through my wallet for Fiona's phone number, then entered my phone card number correctly only on the third try—right before the phone has to electronically arrest and incarcerate you for Attempted Fraud. I said straight off, when Fiona answered, that I promised I'd come see her pieces at the truck gallery tomorrow, when I got back.

"Where are you?" she asked. "I can barely hear you."

"I'm at a Dead show up in Sonora. Things went really badly with Mo."

I told her about Mo's dad's letter, and the fight we got in. "I'm still trying to find him," I explained. "But how *was* your opening? I mean, was it just great?"

"It was okay, Ray. I sold that moose piece, and my dad came."

"Your dad? That's huge, right?"

"It was pretty huge."

I could tell she wasn't all with me, so I told her I simply hadn't been able to get home in time, but that when I could, maybe we'd drive down through Baja together, down to Todos Santos. I promised to do anything, to pay for all the gas and food and even do all the driving. On the way down, we'd go to these hot springs where the eastern Sierra drops to high sagebrush desert. We'd drive out this long dirt road and there'd be cows everywhere and bristlecone pines—the oldest living things on earth. The spring water bubbled up from an underground lake of lava, and when the sun set a holocaust violet behind the skeletal fingers of the Minaret Range, the tub would seem a luminous expression of the fires below. (When there with Mo in the old days— I naturally did *not* tell Fiona—I'd invariably turned to him, naked in all that solitude and glory, and said, "Boy, what could be better, except for you to morph into a beautiful woman?" "Or you," he'd usually said back. "Nah, you," I'd answered.) I told Fiona how we should head down through bleak northern Baja, along perfect blue Magdalena Bay and Scammon's Lagoon, where the gray whales winter after their waterborne journey along precisely the Alaska-to-Baja route we'd be driving. Then, after weeks of silence on endless, empty beaches beneath circling frigate birds, we'd come beneath the elegant purple escarpment of the Sierra de La Laguna, and into the ancient town of Todos Santos, where we'd fish for dorado with handlines, hike silent desert canyons, and wait for the world to change.

"Ray."

Mm?

"Are you on drugs?"

Shit.

"Well?"

"I just know how much you're wondering what's next, and how you're worried about going back to Brooklyn, and you were saying about that church, so I thought . . ."

"You're tripping, aren't you?"

"Everything I said is true, though. I mean, we could really do all that."

There was a long pause, and then Fiona told me I ought to go find Mo. I didn't know why it mattered to her one way or another, but that's what she said. And then she just got off the phone, like she was mad or something. Which perplexed my then-feeble mind and left me preoccupied by my sunburn, my sore knees, and my crooked teeth chipping against each other. I dropped the phone and walked past Evan. In the dirt again, by that chicken-wire fence, I curled up in a ball and wondered if my brain would ever recover the delicious peace of rationally patterned, controlled thought— imagined explaining to my mom that I had to move back home because I was, yes, insane and could never climb the Big Stone or apologize to Mo and would have to stand shamefacedly incoherent beside Evan in his earnest wedding. And that brought me to a vision of the future I was in the process of manifesting: an emotional version of eggs-at-the-base-of-the-throat signifying that my life would come to a screeching halt in a place utterly without referent, a house younger than its occupants on a cul-de-sac of variations on a modest ranch-style theme, and that I'd accept it. I'd yield to a prison of synthetic carpets and endless streams of low-fat frozen cheeseburgers and nonfat ice cream devoured with increasing fatigue before a large-screen TV eternally on the shopping channel, with a man on the air in a matching athletic suit and white sneakers eternally selling home treadmills to people who'd never use them, a man delighted to announce that one might never have to go outside for a walk again. His whole squishy, Styrofoamy, hemorrhoidal world would beam into me, telling me that I, too, needed to keep all my walking within Masonite walls behind drawn fire-retardant blinds with the heat on even on lovely, sunny days as I tried to remember who I was and why I'd come and what there had once been to live for. But the chip implant in my brain and its slow-release rage-suppressant medication (which itself caused that eggy-throat feeling) would keep me sitting on the synthetic pillows under a heap of synthetic blankets (although I wouldn't be cold) as I waited and tried to hear the words escaping the only half-sealed well in which all my horrified possible selves screeched and clawed each other's eyes out in gelatinous hormonal smoke amid a pressing suspicion that I'd actually had some inconsequential bicycle accident causing irreparable brain damage that nobody'd told me about for fear of destabilizing my emotions and that would turn out to have rendered me incapable of anything more than sweeping sidewalks, which I'd now have been hired to do at a local grammar school (and even that only with regular retraining), all a more than twenty-minute drive from the nearest mini-mart, which would be staffed, of course, by ironic, suicidal teenagers through whom I would—as the rage clotted ever more in my throat over the vacant years—turn to mystical religions as embodied in adolescent rock and roll. And then, amidst all those costumed children in the Sierra foothills night, my pea-sized brain just vanished in my auditorium-sized skull, which was filled with foul fog, and my attempts to speak the ultimate aloneness of all humans left that pea-sized brain only to filter for long minutes across that horrible skull void to the lips and emerge as a barely formed "Wow" that promptly got lost as a microscopic collection of unconnected letters, my soul's capacity to interpret experience forever destroyed, the awesome ordering power of the human self only finally clear to me in its absence.

Mushrooms oozed out of my brain in a slow-dripping ecstatic relief as I lay on Evan's cabin floor after the show. I panicked while trying to follow the reasoned thoughts in a three-year-old *Time* magazine; it took four readings to digest each sentence and, once digested, they vanished promptly from memory. I figured that if I had destroyed my capacity to process text—to think in orderly language—I might as well drive off a cliff. But, gradually, elation took over as comprehension grew: *I'm sane! I'm sane!* I slept badly and bolted upright at dawn with a thermonuclear headache, stiff from a hard bed and bewildered from my mind's endless, dreaming replay of sloppy rock and roll and vomiting teenagers and that awful, awful vision of the pass to which my life was coming. I knew Mo'd gone straight to Yosemite after all, and Fiona seemed to understand that I needed to be gone a little longer, so I decided to head up there myself.

With a quick farewell to still-sleeping Evan—who roused only enough to make me promise I wouldn't die before his wedding—I walked into the pine-scented air and got in my truck. Bounced down the dirt ranch road on that silent Sunday morning, through open oak savanna sprinkled with volcanic stones from the ancient fires that had made the mountains: great resource for home rock gardeners like Fiona's dad, who, even now, was probably staring out his big home's kitchen window and dreaming not of the fourteen hundred budding arboreal lives he intended to faithfully clip and coach into figures of this world's serene perfection—not of the Pueblo sandpainting he'd make with Japanese forms in rock and gravel and grass—but of his dead wife. On the highway, a surprising number of out-of-state fire crews headed up smaller roads into the mountains—one from Bend, Oregon, and another from Winnemucca, Nevada.

Psilocybin still fogged my head as I drove, and the radio announced that fifty years of bad forest management had left enough dried underbrush, dead logs, and general kindling to send most of these forests into flames. Lightning strikes had touched off the blaze, and they were already turning people back at the Yosemite park gates. The world seemed changed as I drove up toward

Yosemite—I'd hoped to see some High Sierra vistas, but couldn't on account of all the fire smoke. Even in the taller forest of cedar and sugar pine, with their great smells and cold air, a brown haze obscured the world like earthen fog. Instead of tourists buying sodas at Buck Meadows, three yellow fire trucks waited to refuel. Not a single car crowded the Rim o' the World overlook, and a huge column of ash rose like a mushroom cloud into a blurry sky.

At noon, I passed a few cars headed out of the mountains driven by people with scared, purposeful faces already formulating the great yarns they'd spin at home about how they'd fled before the inferno. At the park entrance itself—just a kiosk in the evergreens, still far from Yosemite Valley itself—more cars waited in the exit lane. A sign read PARK CLOSED DUE TO FIRES, NO ADMITTANCE. I stopped by the side of the road and got out. Stood below a hundred-foot tree, looking into the forest. No fire in there. No bears either, at least not right in front of me. Then I walked over to the ranger kiosk to see if they'd make any exceptions. The old Yosemite Indian ranger was there—rumored to have gorgeous twin daughters both married to famous climbers. He had the sweet grace of an ancient monk, and he'd talk to you for twenty minutes even with a hundred cars in line behind you, but he was also a stickler for form. He could easily have just said no and sent me home and that would have been that. I stood next to his kiosk while he chatted with exiting drivers, but he never turned around. I must have waited half an hour, and the guy just completely ignored me. So I went back to the entrance lane, lifted up the bar, and drove into the park.

From there, at about seven thousand feet, you begin the descent into Yosemite Valley itself. Winding for miles down into that big pit, the road curved along the undulations of the mountainsides. Orange flames glowed beneath a distant black tower of smoke, and a sweating road crew cleared brush along the highway shoulder. At the classic postcard view of the Valley, smoke gave the sheer towers, spires, and walls the aura of dead kings in a tomb. When the road hit the Valley floor, I stopped. Before facing El Capitan up close, I wanted to swim in the Merced and wash off the previous night. In cold pools beside silvery slabs reflecting a pale and diffused sun, I sank under to lie on the river stones like a trout beating upstream. When I lifted my streaming head back into the atmosphere, a coyote slinked along the river grass looking like he'd lost a schoolyard fight. After drying in a meadow devoid of flowers, I drove on through the forest. Curving slowly among the tall trees and over little bridges, I felt deep underground, with those indistinct precipices and their ceiling of smoke blocking the surface world above.

Then, I rounded a bend among normal trees full of birds and squirrels, and there it was, opposite the rocks and spires of the Cathedral group: El Capitan, that white shaft of the planet's raw material jutting into the smoke-thickened skies, a flesh-toned pluto-igneous diamond half a mile long and three thousand feet high—less a static *thing* than an instant in geological time, a flower blooming in a millennial spring. A flock of black cranes dreamt along the creek bank beside me, bending and slow-dancing among the last grasses of their sanctuary's season, doubtless already feeling the cool in their veins, musing on some home deep in the south. Again facing the thing-in-itself, I thought, The hell with mountaineering. El Cap wasn't about mountaineering. As far as I was concerned, El Cap belonged right up there in the same cosmic top ten— the same ontological short list—as the Hagia Sophia, Joyce's *Ulysses*, the hypothetical tenth planet, continental subduction zones, and, well, you get the point. It *counted*. I mean, I can't possibly communicate its real size in words—you'll just have to go see it someday. And don't think you'll understand from a photograph or from a road far away. Go join the Japanese mountaineers, earnest Welsh film crews, and migrant Guatemalan apple pickers, the middle-class Californians on their twelfth trip that year, the road-tripping Kansan families seeing the West with flatlanders' eyes, laughing Polish grandmothers and touring Tibetan monks gathering daily in fresh combinations of our endlessly varied humanity just to bend their necks back and stare, and stare, and feel vaguely unsure of why they are staring. Join them in awe of something far more sublime than Europe's finest temples or Asia's grandest palaces: an utterly American and utterly amnesiac God. And then ask someone to point out a climber lost three or four days into the wall's sheer verticality. Trace the climbing route from the Heart Ledges and Hollow Flake to the Ear, to El Cap Spire, and then to a little colored dot dangling where the mysterious final headwall looms vague in the carbon clouds. You'll feel the same strange sinking in your gut—a kind of spiritual vertigo—that I felt just then as I sighted the minute speck that could only be Mo himself, hanging below the Heart Ledges—a recreational Prometheus no more than a single grain of salt dissolving in an endless freshwater sea.

I sat a long time on a log, pulling up pieces of grass and watching Mo and his two partners work away. Climbing's not much of a spectator sport at close range; from afar, it's a downright bore. All I could do was wonder who these new jokers were and wish Mo hadn't deserted me. I drove over to the dirt turnout below the wall and inspected their VW bus. It was a predictable climber/Dead combo—covered with silly stickers and full of both serious technical hardware and ridiculous fabrics. I pictured having to see Mo when he got down, and having to hear all about how great the climb was, and how cool his partners had been. I pictured the palpable glow of calm self-knowledge Mo would have acquired, and how I'd feel like an untested kid by comparison. I couldn't possibly drive the two hundred and fifty miles home just then, so I decided to spend the night at Camp Four.

I drove past the lesser walls of our early apprenticeship—past the flying buttresses of the Nutcracker Suite and the Five Open Books, all-day routes like East Buttress of Middle Cathedral Rock and the elegant Higher Cathedral Spire, and even the grand Royal Arches, on top of which we'd built a bonfire in the little forest known as the Jungle. Below our first overnight climb, Washington Column, I remembered with pleasure how we'd hauled a Chicago-style deep-dish pizza up to our bivouac ledge, and below Half Dome, our biggest successful climb, I remembered only how frightened I'd been when we'd finished: no excuses left, no more practice climbs before El Capitan. It was pretty depressing to be there again: a kind of retrograde motion of the soul, as though I were stuck in some eddy, incapable of mustering the strength or the will to drag myself out. I rounded the institutional lodge area and parked in the dusty campground lot. I couldn't believe old Raffi's van was still there— that little mobile shrine parked in the forest, a sacred place guys were afraid to approach.

I tried calling Fiona again, but I got her dad's sad voice. I felt too embarrassed to introduce myself or leave a message, so I said I'd call back later. Then I headed over to that climber's purgatory where I'd once imagined I'd gone native forever, now felt like a tourist. Camp Four took up a forlorn plot of gallery forest, with big trees and a dirt floor making a woodland hall full of tents, carved-up picnic tables, and garbage. A cottage-sized boulder in the middle of the campground had a lightning bolt etched into its lichen, marking a terrifically hard sequence of moves called Midnight Lightning. Mo and some guys had cut finger-sized holes out of boards and bolted them to nearby trees for grip training, like that thing on Yabber's van. These boards still hung in the trees, and somebody'd also tied slack lines between stumps for balance practice. Back in the woods, a shantytown of blue tarps and milk crates housed most of the Search and Rescue guys—practicing simplicity and poverty—but I didn't see Yabber around. Three gaunt Europeans sat at a picnic table with a dazed, back-from-the-wars look in their eyes: foreign penitents, there to suffer. Two well-worn haul bags lay on the pine needles nearby.

The place was nearly empty from the evacuation, but all the hard-core climbers and a few tourists had figured out that things weren't so dire just yet. I needed rest, so I claimed a site next door to a very nice married couple from Southern California, Army helicopter mechanics loaded with obsolete camping gear from their base's dispensary. They told me they'd thought Yosemite would be real wilderness; they felt pretty let down. This made me sad, but they hadn't even walked a mile from the road. A scavenging squirrel watched me set up the little happy hermit's life I kept available in the truck at all times: blue single-man tent, red sleeping bag inside, pot and stove neatly out on the table, water bag hung from a tree limb. A lanky blond kid from Vancouver dropped by to say hello, asked right off if I'd climbed El Cap. The kind of kid we'd often seen here: drifting in from some faraway town without explanation, looking to erase any lingering self-doubt. Sitting on my picnic table and eating a strawberry Pop-tart, he said in a teenage dope smoker's voice, "I got to get up on the Captain. Damn, I don't know why . . . It's just like, the Heart? Sheeit . . ." The guy didn't just want the summit, he lusted after every legendary feature—"Ooooh," he said with bedroom eyes in the pine-needle-silenced afternoon, "Hollow Flake? The Ear? The Headwall?" He made a pumping gesture in front of his groin with a chalky hand, a spurting noise with his mouth. "But God *damn*," he muttered over his sweetened lard-plus-starch. "I gotta get up on a wall. I don't know." He shook his head. "I want to *moan*, you know?"

Moan. I want to moan. I wondered if I could possibly do the stone with this guy. The gear was all ready to go, except for those ruined shoes. A raven landed on a crumb-covered table. The Vancouver Vulgarian's girlfriend, a stocky woman with her hair up in a bandanna, handed me a beer. It was her twentieth birthday and she couldn't believe she was in the mountains. A year ago, she said, she'd fallen asleep at the wheel of her car and flipped into a ditch, breaking her C1 vertebrae in three places, C7 in four. Broke a friend's back, too, and they didn't talk much anymore, but she didn't want to talk to that friend anyway. I finished the beer and wished the woman a happy birthday, then decided to nap off my psilocybin shivers.

I climbed in my tent for privacy, but left the door open. Slept right through to Monday morning: fourteen hours' bliss in a cozy goose-down and nylon world. I woke up disoriented by a dream about being aboard a plummeting 747 over a dark northern European nation. The plane had seemed to accelerate toward a blacked-out industrial city at full throttle, with sleet thrashing the windows and cabin lights dead and nobody screaming. Now, I pulled on jeans, washed up in the handicapped outhouse (clean, heated, private), and said good morning to my sweet soldiers and their matching enameled cook pots and coffee kettle—the kind you'd load on the back of a mule if you were going prospecting. I took a pro forma stone's throw at a rogue squirrel, missed as per usual, then walked across the road to get breakfast before driving home. Two does grazed in the meadow's mist, and two turgid red Indian paintbrushes bloomed in the tall grass. I found a pay phone and called Fiona again, but got no answer. Then I called Evan. As it turned out, he'd gone for milk when he got back to town just to have a look at Fiona. He couldn't believe what a catch she was: great looking, but also that aura she had of being a weirdly old soul, at once warm and alive and independently distant. I loved Evan for noticing that—it was exactly why we were friends. He caught me up on his latest wedding dilemmas, too. Still no news from Sloth Ridge Press, though.

When I'd hung up, I walked in the lurking heat of a soon-to-be-sweltering day past the late-season trickle of Yosemite Falls—a dribbling triangular stain across that great granite wall. As I ambled on by, toward breakfast, I felt a pang of sorrow for the poor Bostonian carpet cleaner who'd recently had too many beers in the still warmth above and decided to hang out in the icy shallows of Yosemite Creek. He'd found himself sliding delightfully from pool to pool and then, quite without warning, gliding off the highest waterfall in the United States (roughly the height of Sears Tower). I wondered if he'd ever had a moment's understanding, ever slapped at the beautifully polished granite before taking flight in that most magnificent of skies, rushing honestly and for real toward the ground—*Arruuuga! This is not a test! This is not a test!*—and then splattering like a vine-ripened tomato fired out of a howitzer. Just thinking about it made me dizzy.

At the coffee shop, I joined two obese Mississippian women (shoot me if one wasn't carrying a dog-eared copy of *The Torch and the Tulip*) and a cute little German girl in line. When I finally got a table, Vicky appeared with a smile—a gorgeous, elfin little waitress who'd been working here for years.

"Back already?" she asked. "I thought you were gone forever. Mo with you?"

I told her he was on the Captain even then, probably a couple of pitches into his day.

She smiled at the thought, and shook her head as if to say, That guy's nuts, huh? She'd heard something about Mo riding a bike to Tierra del Fuego, and wanted details, so I told her it was all true. Then I ordered symmetrical, cakey pancakes with balls of fluffed butter and little foil packets of imitation maple syrup. When Vicky'd gone, I read in the *Fresno Bee* how farmers had been caught dumping thousands of undersized peaches on back roads. Then Vicky returned and stood in a hot beam of sun while she made my day by filling my cup from the special staff pot of strong coffee (instead of the brown water they gave tourists). We talked awhile about trivial matters, like people we both knew from working in the park, and about the fires, and how they'd barely been able to keep the highway open. She was worried she wouldn't be able to leave the next weekend—she wanted to visit some friends in Berkeley, see a movie or two, and maybe buy some books. I asked what she'd been doing on her off days, and she told me some of the girls had been bagging lakes together, the way guys bagged peaks. They'd sneak off into the high country after work to skinny-dip in unnamed little alpine tarns.

Full of enough grease and sugar to face the rest of my life, I paid and thanked Vicky and drove along the loop road toward the Big Stone. In the meadow below the wall, that VW was still parked under the oak tree, and at a green minivan two men my age packed a haul bag and arranged hardware. I walked over to talk, tried to hide my jealousy. Asked them to keep an eye out for a party of three above them. One of them looked confident and focused. He turned out to be an East Coast boy, an environmental consultant who'd grown up in D.C. and now lived in San Francisco's Mission District. He had a handsome, mischievous way about him, a wiry build and no apparent fear. His partner was a stocky New Zealander he'd met in a gear store somewhere—in the country to do all the routes his younger sister had done the year before. I just watched them sort gear, then walked out into the meadow. Standing by a dead tree, I easily picked out Mo. Already a hundred feet above the Heart, he worked his way along Lung Ledge toward the Hollow Flake. A German man in leather sandals stood beside me. He said he'd heard people climbed the thing.

"My friend's climbing it right now," I told him.

He refused to believe me, so I borrowed his binoculars and sighted them on Mo for the guy. Except that it wasn't Mo.

I held on to those binoculars longer than was polite just to make sure, focused them carefully on each of the three climbers. There was no mistaking it: Mo was not among them. This was great fucking news. I scanned every other conceivable line on El Cap, and saw nobody on any of them. Just to be certain I hadn't missed something, I drove back to Camp Four and checked the bulletin board. I read every notice offering used gear, every request for a climbing partner or a ride to a distant mountain range, and found nothing from Mo. There was definitely still hope. I quickly wrote a note of my own saying, "Mo, I'm in site #16. Please find me." Then I called Mo's parents to see if they'd heard anything.

Fortunately, I got Mo's mom instead of Old Mo himself. She thought Mo was with me. When I told her what had happened, she was certain this was it, the time Mo'd never come home. I walked around like a moron most of that day, watching likely cars for hitchhikers, looking for Yabber. Checked the bulletin board every few hours, reorganized all the El Cap gear, and just generally had no idea what the hell to do. I badly wanted Mo to show, but if I'd been honest with myself, I would have realized he could have gone anywhere. I did know that if he were in the Valley, he'd go to the old Ahwahnee Hotel at night. So, just after dark, I walked through the quiet forest below the looming monoliths to the grand old lodge and looked around. I didn't see Mo, but the Great Hall had a fireplace and free tea service for guests, so I decided to loiter and enjoy leather upholstery and warm smiles from well-to-do vacationers. Eventually, I got to talking to a honeymooning Spanish couple. The guy did the in-house advertising for an Italian clothing company, she was a dentist's assistant, and they were very much in love. The man was a climber himself, and when I mentioned that I'd come up here to do El Capitan but missed my partner, his eyes got this ardent hunger I understood absolutely, as if El Capitan was simply the grandest, most glorious and romantic adventure possible.

On Tuesday morning, I drank coffee in the dappled sunshine of the campground and tried to keep my breathing even as I looked around in the forest.

Someone in a red jacket walked across the quiet road. I called Evan.

"Ray," he said, "where the hell are you?"

"I'm still in the Valley."

"No sign of Mo, huh?"

"Not yet. I don't think he's here. Any mail I ought to know about?"

"Mm . . . yeah, actually. There is. There's a package from Sloth Ridge."

I took a long breath, looked through the empty Camp Four at swallows bouncing on picnic tables.

"Want me to open it?" Evan asked.

"Sure." I heard him tearing the envelope.

"Shall I read it?"

"Yeah."

"Oh, dude, you sure you want to do this?"

"Bad news?"

"It kind of looks that way."

"Read it."

" 'Dear Mr. Connelly, I'm sorry to tell you that, after long and careful consideration, Sloth Ridge has decided not to publish your work.' "

Evan paused as I exhaled and rubbed my eyes.

"That's pretty straightforward, huh?" I said. "No beating around the bush?"

"You want me to read the rest? It's really short."

"Why not?"

"Okay. 'Although we were initially very excited by your work, we've had an extremely discouraging letter from an outside reader. If you wish to see this letter, I will gladly send you a copy, but for now, suffice to say that it raised reservations far too serious for us to ignore. Thanks very much for sending us your work, and I hope you'll keep us in mind on future projects.' Motherfucker. Motherfucking shit-fucker.''

"Evan."

"Yeah?"

"You really haven't heard anything from Mo?"

"Nope."

There was a long pause, and then I spoke: "Look, I'll call you in a few days, okay?"

"Raymond, man. I'm really sorry about this. I'm serious. I can't imagine what it must . . ."

"I just got to go."

And that was the end of that. Pretty awful, really. I sat on a log for a few minutes trying to slow my breathing, blinking my eyes. Then I tried Fiona at the grocery store.

"Where are you this time?" she asked.

"I'm in Yosemite Valley."

"Why do you keep calling me from these places? Did you work things out with your friend?"

"I can't find him. His dad killed my book, though."

She paused, then asked if there was anything I could still do.

"Like what?"

"Well, just take Mo out of it, or something."

I held the phone away from my head and screamed silently into the forest. There'd be nothing left, I told Fiona, putting the phone back to my face. Mo was the whole book.

She didn't respond.

"You know what I mean?" I asked. "I just wanted to share this great guy with the rest of the world."

"Ray."

"What?"

"That's bullshit."

"How?"

"You know it's more complicated than that."

"How is it more complicated than that?"

"People have a lot invested in their stories." She paused. "Like the one I told you." I heard her breathe slightly, as if her chest were tightening.

"Fiona."

"Yes."

"I haven't told that to a soul."

"Anyway," she said, clearly wanting a change of subject.

"I haven't."

"That's not the point, okay? When are you coming back?"

"It's not . . . Well, maybe as late as next week, but . . ."

"I don't know if I'll be here."

"What do you mean?"

"My plans are just up in the air, that's all. But you knew that."

"I'll probably be back tomorrow night."

"Look, Raymond, I'm at work. I've got to go. Good luck, though, really."

Yabber's van was parked next to my truck—Buddha sunset, mountain bike, finger board and all. He stood there bouncy as ever, cracking his knuckles and talking about the fires and wondering where Mo was. He felt sure Mo'd been on his way up here, couldn't figure out what happened. Feeling pretty sick of my whole predicament—it seemed like virtually everybody was irritated with me—I asked if Yabber'd lead me up the Captain himself. But he was taking some time off. Tried to sell me T-shirts of Yosemite he'd silk-screened right in his VW. I didn't know how not to talk to him, so I looked over the shirts. One had a drawing of the Captain that (he pointed out with heavy implication) was full of faces: smiling theater masks of comedy and tragedy, and monstrous women and scowling fathers and big blades wrapped into the skyline—*very* mysterious. "Like the rocks," Yabber said with a lurid, nervous giggle. After getting off the phone with Fiona, I'd felt as though something had fallen right out of the middle of me, and kept falling, and this eccentric idiot kept rambling about how urban centers were throbbing lesions on an otherwise glorious continent, how he hadn't been to L.A. or San Fran in fifteen years, thought he might never return. Had a whole T-shirt business worked out where he could loiter forever in the park, sponging off tourists and doing the Big Stone. He said this with great glee, as if letting me in on a good scam. I tried not to tell him what I thought of him, or that I seemed to be blowing it with a great woman in order to chase a friend I'd apparently never see again to a place I should've left behind years before.

"Yabber," I said, looking around the tired-out campground. "Introduce me to Raffi." Late summer had exhausted all its hot breath.

"I'm not really tight with Raffi anymore."

"Tell him I just need my shoes repaired."

Yabber said Raffi was full of shit, and that I shouldn't pay too much attention to his ramblings. But he also agreed to take me over. As I followed Yabber across the dusty parking lot, the Valley seemed tawdry under its blanket of organic smog. The midmorning sun blurred into a broad ball. I couldn't help but wonder what in God's name I was going to do with the rest of my life. In the far corner of the lot, in a grove of big old oak trees, Raffi's red van rested on blocks. In the diffuse shade of an oak, the van had one bumpersticker: "Gravity: It's the Law." Raffi himself, the original Deep Space Ranger, was apparently inside the van.

Yabber stepped forward, spoke a few words, and then waved me over. I couldn't believe the old hero was actually going to talk to me. When Yabber disappeared, I noticed that the woman from the concert sat peacefully on a milk crate outside Raffi's van. Her eyes were closed—the eyes that had seemed pretty infernal that night at the show. Her lips moved slightly as if she were singing, and she had one hand inside a leather pouch that hung from her neck by a string. Just the sight of her gave me grisly little quivers of neural nightmare memory, but she didn't recognize me, which was a huge relief. She just smiled faintly and walked away. I heard an electric grinding sound inside the van, and smelled burnt rubber. A wooden rack stood nearby with old climbing shoes dangling from pegs. On the ground, a crate held a few more filthy pairs. There were scraps of black rubber everywhere. Swallows fiddled in a big oak. The door of the van was open, and I could see the immaculately organized interior, with colorful illustrations around a wooden altar and a jar of wilted wildflowers. Tools hung from handmade holders, and a leather pouch dangled from the rearview mirror.

Then Raffi stepped out holding a pair of black

iron pliers, the blades of which were wide and sharp and curved apart like black wings. He wore cheap rubber sandals and clean old jeans. He didn't meet my eyes at first, just looked lazily past me. He rubbed his leathery face with the back of his hand and rolled his head around, popping several vertebrae in his neck. A bird picked around in the yellow flowers near his simian toes, and Raffi's mouth drooped slightly as if he were lost inside himself. Though his body looked light and strong, Raffi's eyelids hung like those of an old alcoholic.

I gestured to my shoes. "I know you don't really do this, but . . ."

Half asleep, he gestured to an old car seat propped against that oak. "Sit down, if you like." So I sat, lonely enough to appreciate the offer. Raffi looked at me awhile, rubbed a knee, and then leaned back into the open doorway of the van. He lit a stick of incense on the flame of an oil lamp. Then he pulled up that milk crate and sat, too.

"I'm just wondering if there's any way you could do a half sole," I asked, "just from the instep forward. The rands are fine, and the midsole's probably okay. It shouldn't be a big deal."

He listened vacantly and turned my shoes in his hands, looked at the sole of each. "You in a hurry?" he asked, still not looking at me.

"No, not really. Pretty much nowhere I need to be, ever."

He nodded vaguely, then cleared his throat. "Yabber tells me you know old Mo Lehrman."

I nodded, guessed I did.

Raffi reached into the van and hauled out a waist-high post with a foot-shaped iron last on top.

"If you do it today," I asked, "how much will it cost?" Thirty dollars would have been a fair price; twenty would have been generous.

He didn't answer, just loosened the laces of my right shoe and stretched it over the jack. He looked as though he'd been terrifically strong once, was now more efficient than powerful. With an industrial strength blow-dryer, Raffi began heating the soles, loosening their remaining glue bonds. A squirrel appeared on a log, and I stared into the forest without focusing, saw Mo's face and El Capitan and Fiona and a lot of branches. I remembered a picture I'd once seen of Raffi in a magazine, on a famous part of the Big Stone. "You've done El Cap a lot, right?" I asked.

His glazed eyes listed over to me. *"Maya."*

"Hm?"

"Illusion."

"What? No, I meant El Cap."

A raven cawed in immense irritation over his head. "Is that why you're up here?" he asked me.

Of course it was.

Raffi set the shoe back in the shade, sat again on his milk crate. The heat bore down, and dust stuck to my sweating neck. I picked up a sharp oak leaf and poked it into the skin of my palm.

Raffi turned and looked at me, holding the heat gun in one hand. "So, what's the problem?"

"What do you mean?"

"You're unfulfilled?"

"What?"

"Well, what do you think El Cap's going to do for you?"

"El Cap?"

"You like to repeat people's questions, don't you?"

"I just didn't . . ."

"You shouldn't do that." With those pliers, he pinched the sole right where it met the shoe and began to pry gently, breaking the bond without tearing the shoe. "You don't have any idea why you want to climb El Cap?" he asked. The sole didn't part just there, so he tried another spot with the pliers.

"I honestly don't. You've done it a lot. You must get something out of it."

He finally broke a section of the bond, freeing a few inches of sole from the shoe. It made me nervous to watch. If he ruined these shoes, I was screwed.

"I chastise myself," Raffi said, not looking at me. "To remain detached. It just feels good because you're satisfying the body." He rubbed a knee impatiently with his free hand. "But you're never fulfilled from climbing. Right?"

I guessed I wasn't.

"You know why?"

Of course not.

"Because you're polishing the car, but you forgot the driver, who didn't do *shit* for himself." He really laid into his words, and the sole began to come away from the shoe now, taking up some of the midsole—just some lousy particle board now reduced to dust.

"But haven't you climbed El Cap about eighty times? I mean, isn't that your thing?"

He squinted at me. "It's not a bona fide process. Has to be bona fide. What I mean is, the soul's the real owner—that's the real person within the body. The body's just the body." He put the other shoe on the jack now, turned the heat gun on it. "The soul's always blissful," he said, still heating, "but it's covered by the body, like the sun's covered by clouds, so you think, 'Now I'm suffering, now I'm happy, now I'm an American, now I'm a stool-eating hog.' You see how the coverings are? So, you get that little blissfulness when you climb, like maybe you think you'll conquer your fear of death." The rubber began to bubble from the heat. He put down the heat gun and began to pry up the right sole.

That woman, quite beautiful in her blue shorts and tank top, stood nearby and smiled obsequiously. I really hated seeing her—my stomach clenched and my head got swimmy and weak. I asked if I should leave. Raffi shook his head.

"No really," I said. "I don't mind."

"Stay." Then he turned to the woman and asked what she wanted.

"Well, I'm going hiking on the Four Mile Trail,

but I want to talk to you a little." She stood a few paces off.

"I'll be here."

"What time? Because, we really do have to talk about some things."

"I'll be here."

I could see Yabber waiting for her by his bus. He gave Raffi a look that seemed to say, I told you so.

"We'll talk to you later, kid," Raffi said, not looking at her. As she walked off, Raffi pried away at that sole. A jay bounced among pointed oak leaves on the ground.

Then Raffi reached back into the van and pulled out a three-foot-square sheet of shiny black rubber. With a white pencil, he traced both shoe outlines like corpses on pavement. I looked around at the trees and the walls above it all, the birds and the quiet broken only by the occasional fire truck and helicopter. Raffi dipped a green-handled knife into a paper cup full of water, then he drew its worn blade through the rubber as if through warm flesh. A new set of thunderheads appeared down-valley, and ice cream sounded fine—a whole lot of it, in a bright red flavor, like strawberry.

When he'd cut two new soles, Raffi took them and the shoes into the van. He turned on that grinder and roughened all the surfaces to be glued.

"The problem is also where you are," Raffi said, stepping back outside and brushing rubber dust from his hair and face.

"Yeah?"

"Yeah. Everything is fallen in this Age of Kali. This is a very bad age. Very hard for the heart to develop its God-consciousness. Because that's what it is."

"That's what what is?"

"What's in your heart. God-consciousness." He brushed all the sanding dust off my shoes and the new soles, then opened a tin of toluene. "And this is the worst place," he said. "*Kali*fornia. Farther west, the more the sinful entity lives." He poured toluene on a red rag, and began to wipe it along all the surfaces to remove any oils that might weaken the glue bond. It stained the rubber a darker black, but then it evaporated as if it had never been there.

"Yeah," I said, "you go west from here, you get to India."

"You get to Hawaii."

"I know, I just . . ."

"Hawaii's not a continent."

"I mean you go to the next continent, and you're in India . . ."

"No." He opened a tin of toluene-based glue and, breathing deeply, brushed the water-thin fluid onto the shoes and soles.

"Well, sure. You get to India. In fact . . ."

"In India, people are more pure."

Raffi set all the glued surfaces to dry in the sun. Lighting a stick of incense from a small oil lamp inside the van, he said the drying would take an hour.

I passed the drying time lying in a meadow while the wildfires burned and everyone hoped for rain. Maybe Raffi was right. No way around the fact that something very crummy had developed in my heart, nor that El Cap had offered itself as a balm. Nor could I deny that, while I'd never met a genuinely happy climber, much of the world seemed to derive lasting relief from some kind of God-consciousness. When I returned to the parking lot two hours later with a Coke and two Snickers bars, my shoes and soles were still drying outside Raffi's van. I heard a soft ringing, as if from a bell. Inside his van, Raffi knelt on an Ensolite pad, eating almonds and reading from a small yellow book.

"Hi," I said, popping open that Coke. "Probably dry now, huh?" I opened one of the Snickers bars.

He nodded, not looking at me. Then he set aside the book and washed down the last of his food with a gulp of water. The guy was in no hurry at all. He seemed to have decided in some bloody recess of his brain that this redheaded youth needed to be delayed. Stepping into the sun, he pressed a fingernail against one of the glued surfaces to see that all the solvent had evaporated.

"Ready to go?" I asked.

Raffi glanced sideways at my Snickers, then pulled that heat gun out of the van again. He ran it over one shoe and one sole. When the glued surfaces were hot, he aligned the new soles and pressed them down hard. Steadying each shoe with one hand, he pounded the soles with a piton hammer to bind the glue. After twenty strokes, he paused to breathe. While he worked, I sat again on that car seat and enjoyed the chocolate, the chewy nougat, and the nuts; swilled a little Coca-Cola. When Raffi was done pounding, he sat again, waiting for the bond to cure before he could trim off the excess rubber. I looked into the sky, but saw nothing. A jay picked at the tiny dust-filled carcass of a swallow chick that had died on its maiden voyage. I mulled over what Fiona had said to me about her story— something about it made me uncomfortable, and I watched cars and motorcycles anxiously, looking for that big Mo Lehrman head. The air seemed awkwardly neutral, with that holocaust in the mountains now getting fanned by an Aleutian low pressure bearing upon us from the north. I caught Raffi looking at my Snickers bar just then, and asked if he'd like one.

He looked at the wrapped candy bar in my hand, then around the parking lot. We sat low, out of sight of the other parked cars. "Sure," he said. "You want some milk?"

"You kidding?"

He grabbed a quart from his van, opened it, and handed it to me. He looked pretty pleased about all that chocolate and chewy nougat.

"Hey," I asked. "Aren't those shoes cured yet?"

He stood and picked one up. He tugged at the excess sole and watched the glue bond. The white fibers stretched slightly. "Not dry yet," he said. "But I could finish them now anyway."

"No, no."

"I mean, if you don't care about your soles staying on, then why not?"

"Sorry," I said. "Let's wait."

Two big prop planes pounded overhead, full of water to dump on the fires. Raffi spilled milk on his chin as he gulped. Then he tested the glue bonds again, and this time they did not stretch. He reached into the van for that cup of water and a hook-billed drawknife.

I guess I looked as bewildered as I felt, because as Raffi cradled one of the shoes against his chest, he started talking again. "What I'm trying to tell you," he said, "is that climbing El Cap is not what you need."

"No?"

"No. You have to meditate to awaken your God-consciousness, and you can't meditate on void, on nothing, like Buddhists. The negation of material activities only comes to neutrality, which means zero, where the soul is inactive. Samtanarasa, zero—nirvana. You stay there, you fall back down to the material side, due to not having any *engagement*. To escape suffering, you have to meditate on a concrete process, something you can grasp, otherwise you go crazy after a while. The process *has* to come from God, not just from any speculator who says, 'Well, we'll do this process,' like so-called Yogic systems. 'Like, I'll climb a mountain and see God.' The Lord is the Creator, so He knows perfectly well what is good for you to meditate on, and if you talk to God, and He's a person, then it's a very nice thing, here. Right?"

I nodded: right.

"That's a pretty damn good candy bar," Raffi said, looking at the wrapper. Then he set it down and dipped the drawknife into the water. He sliced along the white glue line at the shoe's edge, trimming off the excess the way you'd skin an apple. "But, anyway, if you don't talk to God, and you become an ass in this life, in your next life, you'll just become an ass in the field, maybe one that recites poetry, but who cares? Who listens? This is what causes climbers to fall. They get all puffed up, and prideful with a doggish mentality, and then in your next life, you'll be a dog in Camp Four. Here, nice doggy-doggy. Then you bark too much and they throw bottles at you, and the dog's always chained to the master. But if you're God's dog, and live the life you're meant for, that's calling inside you, then the master will be nice. So, you'd rather be Krishna's dog then some mundane master's dog." Raffi turned and called out to a hairy climber pissing in the trees. "Come on, man! I've got to work back here!"

"I already started!" the guy said quite apologetically, shuffling behind another tree.

"I'm not kidding," Raffi said, pointing at him with that knife, "that's bullshit. I got to work back here every day." The guy zipped up, pleaded forgiveness, and walked off. A dog nibbled at something near a garbage can—me in my next life, perhaps. I looked down-valley toward the Captain. Raffi stepped back into the van now, and turned on the generator again. I stood up and leaned against its open door. "So," he said, in a far lighter tone— as if he'd changed subjects—"this logic isn't mine. I've been studying it."

"Yeah?"

"Yeah." He drew the shiny edge of the new sole along the sanding belt, smoothing the glue seam and softening the angle of the sole's edge. He paused for a moment and handed me that small yellow book he'd been reading. "This is Krishna Consciousness of the International Society of Krishna Consciousness," he told me, sanding the bottoms of the shoes now, roughing the rubber for better friction against rock, "of A. C. Bhaktivedanta Swami Prabhupada going through Lord Caitanya to Madhvacaray, then to Brahma and all the way back to the Lord himself. And the Lord has a name. It's Morinda, Krishna. According to his activity. Ultimately he has no name, but he has names according to his activities. Not Shiva, not Vama—Shiva and Vama demigods. Not bona fide. Krishna means all-attractive one. Over here they call them the Hare Krishnas. Because Hare is the energy, Krishna is the Lord, so the more you chant, the more it dances on your tongue, the more the holy Names manifests itself. When you become pure enough, the Lord himself comes and dances on your tongue, and vibrates the Holy Names, otherwise, if you're not pure enough, God doesn't come." He stepped out of the van. "Someone who knows," he continued, "is very, very rare in this age. And even if someone knows just a little bit, then there's levels. Compared to the real liberated souls, I know nothing. I'm just giving you the ABC's. The real liberated souls have entered into the real mystery. Although, it's not a mystery, anyway."

The woman appeared again, standing outside our presumed sphere of intimacy. She didn't seem to have gone hiking at all—still too clean. I stepped back under the oak to let her talk to him, and to look at the book, *A Beginner's Guide to Krsna Consciousness*, by Bhakti Vikasa Swami. On the back cover, it said,

Read This Book and Improve Your Life! All you need to know to get started in Krsna consciousness. Easy-

to-understand guidance on daily practices that bring us closer to Krsna. Packed with practical information. Suitable for devotees living at home or in an asrama.

- *How to meditate*
- *Home worship*
- *Recognizing and accepting a bona fide guru*
- *Purified eating*
- *Bhajanas*
- *Observing festivals and vows*
- *Acquiring transcendental knowledge*
- *And many other details of the Krsna success formula that has satisfied millions of devotees throughout the world*

Guaranteed to make you a better, more spiritual person.

I had to admit, it sounded great. Raffi shook my hand softly and slowly, looking at me with those pale blue eyes. His hand felt at once steel-hard and gentle, and his skin was coarse and very dry. Over his shoulder, he agreed with the woman about something. She was in the van, writing on a piece of paper.

I inquired about the price of the resole.

"It's okay," he said, handing me the piece of paper. "You going home in the morning?"

I had no idea.

"Well, for when you get back, there's the number of the Vaishnava Community where you live.

Just call Jagarini devi after twelve noon and at least go for the free vegetarian dinner."

I looked at the paper. It was that place by the park. Somewhat dazed, I thanked Raffi and walked across the parking lot with my renewed shoes and my new book, and the promise of a free meal in San Francisco. As I passed Yabber's van, Buddha still floated in perfect serenity over that blue sunset, meditating on nothing.

Yabber called out to me: "I bought something for you, Raymond."

I stopped walking, stood in the heat and dust. The sun had fallen behind the evergreens, and they seemed loopy and frail in silhouette.

Yabber reached across his bedding, then rolled out of the van with a blue plastic baggie. He handed it to me with a faint grin on his sun-creased face.

"Yabber, I'm not in the mood for . . ."

"Look inside."

"Honestly."

"It's not what you think."

And it wasn't. The little sack was full of Jolly Ranchers.

Mo woke me at midnight. Such a big, wild guy, so raw and sweet and searching. He blinked his blackened eye and smiled faintly when I pointed my flashlight at him. I smiled back and rubbed my own eyes, pulled an arm out of my sleeping bag to shake hands. I got pine needles all over my wool socks as I pulled on my jeans.

"Hi," he said in his tentative, inquisitive way. He smelled drunk, bobbed his head as he looked around in the darkness. There was a look in his eyes I didn't recognize.

When we'd stared at each other for a moment, I asked where he'd been.

"Mm, around." Mo looked me up and down,

like a mom checking her daughter's rain jacket in a squall. "What're you reading?"

The little yellow book lay on the ground. I handed it to Mo.

"Raffi?" he asked.

"How'd you know?"

"I told you that guy was a kook."

"Mo," I said again, trying to wake up, "where you been?"

"Just doing some stuff." He shoved his hands deep in his pockets, then looked over his shoulder into the blackness of the forest. Someone was washing pots in the bathroom. "Get your climbing shoes back?"

"Yeah, I got them."

"Pretty wrecked?"

"Raffi fixed them this afternoon. No charge."

"You want to climb?"

Nothing moved in all that sacred, secret ground of Camp Four. I reached down for my sleeping bag. "Probably suck, you know?"

Mo smiled. "It'll definitely suck."

"De facto, it will be miserable."

We were both laughing now. "Just go climbing?"

"Yeah, little rock climbing."

"You and me?"

"Yeah, little climbing."

I broke down my tent and stuffed my sleeping bag, and then we pulled my truck around to the fluorescent lights of the closed gas station. It was too late for me to call Fiona's home, but while Mo pulled out our gear, I did call Evan's voice mail and leave a message saying I'd try to be back for the wedding, and might even be able to bring Mo along.

Mo wanted, as usual, to bring virtually nothing: no weather radio, no bolt-drilling kit for self-rescue, no extra set of rain gear. I wanted, as usual, to bring all of the above, and more. Mo wanted to skip the extra food and water, even to go light on our alloted rations; I suggested several days' extra. On item after item, Mo won. He felt, as always, that if you overprepared, you doomed yourself; better to have faith in the universe, and thereby win its benevolence. My heart rambled and I had to breathe deeply to keep from panicking. Mo sensed this, and stopped talking to me. Told me to take all twenty of those duct-tape armored, two-liter Coke bottles to a spigot and refill them—the water from the warehouse would be pretty ripe by now. I stood in the buzzing pale light among mosquitoes and moths, pouring water into the containers and trying to stay calm. The hardware was already organized in its milk crate, so Mo just had to pack the haul bag. When I was done with the water, we stood the bag upright and began loading in the water bottles. All the canned food went in next, then four liters of Christian Brothers Burgundy and Mo's bottle of aspirin, and a bunch of pink-and-white Brach's candy bags, each with four squares of toilet paper. We had to work our warm clothes and sundries—our bagels for breakfast and chocolate bars for lunch, and even our sleeping bags—into the remaining cracks and crannies. All told, it came to well over a hundred pounds.

At around three-fifteen a.m., we had the bag crammed full. I held it while Mo jumped on it a few times to get everything settled. Then we hoisted the pig into the back of the truck and drove along the empty loop road under the aspen trees. It felt great to be together in my truck again, in spite of everything.

"Just go do it, huh?" Mo asked. "Just go up and do El Cap?"

Seemed like an awful idea. Suicidal, even.

"Just go climbing?"

We parked directly below the stone—a luminous hole of starless dark filling most of the northern night sky. In the cool air, we put on our climbing clothes and shoes. Mo still wore his Levi's—ridiculously impractical, but his way of saying, "I am not a 'climber,' and this is not a 'climb.' I am merely a human, and this is merely a place." The palms of my hands were very damp. Mo shouldered the padded loop of cord carrying all our hardware: about sixty snap-link carabiners and a forest of friends, hexcentrics, and stoppers. Close to thirty pounds of metal arranged the way it had always been arranged between us: this part was automatic and required no rapprochement. Mo also threw two of the coiled fifty-meter ropes over his shoulders, and carried the third in his arms. Then we stood the haul bag on the end of the truck's tailgate while I squirmed into its shoulder straps. When I leaned forward, my knees gave under the weight. Crossing the road felt like wandering on a planet with far too much gravity.

We entered the quiet forest below the wall then. The footpath wound and bent and looped first among oaks, then into dense willows. Once, we lost our way, had to retrace. As we neared its base, the wall became too big to see—its upper three-quarters lost entirely in foreshortening. The spot of my headlamp bounced across granite cobblestones and fallen tree trunks, picked out the path every wall pilgrim must walk. Ahead, the gear clanked and rattled around Mo. Breathing became quick, and I opened and closed my hands, tried to dry my palms. Sweating and panting from the bag's weight, I stopped several times to rest against trees. No bird sounds. No insect sounds. The obscene presence invisible overhead. At four-thirty a.m., we stood at the base of El Capitan—right where Yabber'd seen that BASE jumper disintegrate at terminal velocity. Most cliffs have some tapering off at the bottom, break into a long slope gradually easing off—they seem a risen part of the earth. El Cap has more the feel of a talismanic monolith of unique origin. A *thing*, too, and not a pile of rubble, dirt, or snow. Just one stone with a maddening meaning-lessness as we stood there among the oaks, tying the laces of our climbing shoes. We wrapped our hands in athletic tape and shouldered day packs full of sunscreen, Pop-Tarts, water, and rain gear. We strapped on knee pads, buckled our harnesses, and clipped chalk bags, nut tools, locking cara-biners, and belay and rappel devices to our harness gear loops. Then we tied ourselves together with a rope. Sitting next to the haul bag, I sucked a long breath. I heard Mo sigh. The beam of his headlamp swept up the stone before us.

"Am I on belay?" he asked.

"You sure you're okay?" I could still smell alcohol on him.

"Oh, yeah." He sighed. "Am I on?"

"You're on belay."

"Climbing." An awkward, poorly feathered bird bristling with gaudy bits of metal.

"Climb." And that was that. He put one hand in the two-inch wide crack that ran out of the ground, and pulled up. My pulse seemed high. As I played out the rope, I kept my knees tight for warmth. Every few feet, Mo lodged a piece of gear in the crack, clipped a carabiner to it, and ran the rope through. About half an hour after he'd begun, I heard soft cursing overhead. Bits of gravel and dirt showered down. I heard Mo mumble.

"Yeah?" I asked.

"Oh . . ." His voice trailed off in distraction.

"Yeah?"

"Just a little interesting here." It's hard to start a big wall like that, with no warming up. One moment you're a creature of the horizontal, of Earl Grey and softboiled eggs. The next, every movement requires perfect athletic focus.

"Yeah?"

"Yeah, a little interesting." His voice hinted at fear. "Ray?"

"Yeah."

"I'm going to fall, okay?"

"Okay," I called up into the darkness. "Go ahead and fall." I locked the rope at my harness. No sound. Then, a grunt overhead, and the rope jerked me a foot off the ground.

Mo hung in the darkness above. I could just hear his breathing. He didn't move.

"You okay?" I asked.

"Just needed to fall, you know?" I heard him blow his nose, felt his weight on my hips and thighs, his life in the palm of my hand.

"Yeah?"

"Yeah. Loosen up a little."

I laughed, relieved.

"Climbing."

"Climb."

After almost an hour, he'd built an anchor—fixed us to the wall for the first time. With the dawn sky fingering burgundy, he called down: "I'm off belay. Rope's fixed." A moment later, he said he was ready to haul.

I tied the second rope to the haul bag and called up, "Haul away."

The rope came taut on the bag, then stretched. Then the bag inched off the ground. It jerked up a few feet and swung. Soon it was gone. I clipped jumars—metal handles with one-way ratchets and nylon foot-stirrups—to the rope, and started upwards. I tried not to look overhead, paused after thirty feet to slow my breathing. The granite was smooth and white, and glinting swaths of polish splashed the setting moon.

When dawn broke bright and yellow across the forest-fringed ramparts of the Cathedral Rocks, we'd gained two hundred feet. There was too much to say, so we talked very little. When we passed the anchor that had once broken, killing those two perfectly nice guys from Fresno, we were still in shadow, but already the day grew hotter. The orderliness of gear became a ritual obeisance to the void, as we carefully coiled every rope, put every piece of equipment in its proper place. By the pale, fire-sickly noon, we thrashed up cracks full of rusted old iron pitons and faces of flattened rivets, stitched our way up this lowest rampart. Occasionally we even had fun—one friction slab felt like a dance floor with each step etched by God into its grain. As I eased past the place where I'd freaked out before—where Mo had yielded to my fear and agreed to go down, poured out all the water and let it blow in the breeze—the swallows found me again. Their malicious squadron of temple guards whipped, snapped, and soared about my head, as if to remind me of the plodding worthlessness of wingless albatrosses like myself. I dropped a carabiner in agitation, my fingers working too quickly. But somehow, this time, I was focused enough not to panic. A black raven also found us. In a few days, we'd be into the higher reaches, inhabited by falcons, but that afternoon only this unkempt scavenger followed us with the patience of the depraved. It perched casually on a tiny flake of stone to my left, and when I moved higher, it rode an updraft to a yet higher perch. Then it cawed with terrible irritation, squawking out a petulant complaint in its raven language.

When next I stood beside Mo, I noticed two small dots far, far above on the final headwall—doubtless that Kiwi and the guy from D.C. Then I saw a third dot. It appeared to be moving. In fact, it appeared to be growing.

"Mo."

"Hm?"

"Something's falling."

He leaned out to look up. It was falling directly toward us, and neither of us wore helmets. Even a small rock could brain us. We couldn't possibly go sideways, and there were no cracks to hide in, no overhangs to duck under. Absolutely nowhere to hide.

"Oh my God," Mo mumbled, his mouth half-open.

We covered our heads and huddled together as the whistling got louder. There was a flapping noise, and then a sudden splatter all around us. Something heavy but soft thumped across my head and hands and neck. Mo howled before I knew what had hit us. I looked around for blood, for shattered rock, and then saw it: there on top of the bag, all over my hands, and throughout both our heads of hair, steamed piles of human shit, incontinent and infirm, the waste of the loose-boweled. Mo stared at me slack-jawed and beyond outrage, lips working to phrase inconceivable indignities. Very little water to spare for cleaning, no grass or sand or paper to wipe with: raw, base humiliation. Before moving to clean anything at all, Mo looked west for a long time, into the blurred and inarticulate atmospheres of the way home. Then he clawed at his befouled hair and screamed murderously at the wayward climbers somewhere overhead. I joined him, and we held our hands out, opened our throats, and shouted homicide. The mood of everything had gone sour, and on a big climb, mood is everything.

"The knife," I said. "Your fucking pocketknife."

Way beyond joking, Mo wiped shit from the back of one hand, and reached into his day pack. He opened his pocketknife and, with clenched teeth, we took turns hacking each other's polluted locks off. The filthy strands dropped into the transverse northwesterly breeze that swept them tumbling and floating down toward the peanut-butter-and-jelly sandwiches of picnicking families. I'd never been so furious. "Let's get out of here," I said, quite seriously.

"You mean go down?"

"Don't you think? I mean, there's no way we can get clean."

Mo opened one of our precious two-liter water bottles, tore off a clean part of his shirt, and started pouring water over me and scrubbing. "No way we're going down," he said. "We'll just drink less."

When we'd cleaned each other best we could, we began climbing again. Then the sun hit us, and the day seemed fully alive. I looked up and got a kick-in-the-stomach weakness in the knees, like standing on a fiftieth-floor balcony of a building half a mile wide and looking up two hundred and fifty more floors. All day, we took turns sitting on ledges—one climbing above or below the other—watched cars leave the Valley, and tried to ignore that raven. We talked very little. The sun had neared the pines along the Valley's north ridge. Mountainous shadows fell across the meadow like tombstone shadows in the desert. When I reached the Heart Ledges at last—our home for the night—I leaned against the wall and waited for Mo. Gear clanked around his shoulder as he dragged himself up, alight with the orange glow of a soft California dusk.

We coiled and organized the ropes and hardware,

then clipped every loose water bottle, sleeping bag, day pack, shirt, and shoe to the wall until the ledge looked like a tenement yard. We pulled off our climbing shoes and rested—no drama, and much peace. Raffi's soles had held up fine. Smoke blurred dusk into a sluggish river of yellow and crimson—incense twirling in a burnt offering. As night fell, a tiny flashlight walked home across the broad meadow. Though a simple stumble could have killed him, Mo refused to tie himself to our anchor bolts and scoffed at my nervousness. We put on sweaters and drank the first liter of wine, ate cans of beef chili. It was wonderful to forget—to be nothing but a soul in space. At dark, I heard that solitary raven's brittle caw again, the bird still pursuing its idle errand in the trees. As we spread out our sleeping bags, the beams of our headlamps shrank the world to our little sphere of light. I looked away from the wall once, but then my headlight's beam just vanished sickeningly, as though there were no more world. Lying and waiting to sleep, knowing how much work and uncertainty lay ahead, I tried to chat. Asked Mo what he was doing next, if he was coming to Evan's wedding or not.

"They're pretty in love, huh?"

"Yeah, Evan's lucky."

"That's great. Howbout your girl?"

I was getting worried about that. "I don't know, Mo. I probably shouldn't have come to the warehouse that night."

"What's she like?"

"We only went out a couple times, so who knows? Maybe we'd hate each other. But there's something about her I never felt with Susan."

"Oh, man, you were pretty sweet on Susan. I liked her."

"I guess I shouldn't say that. It's just this weird vitality Fiona has, you know? She does it for me. I haven't been around a woman like that in a long time."

Standing at the ledge's edge, Mo asked if I had a "Great Pisses I've Taken" memory bank. "Devoted just to that? Like this whole part of your brain?" He giggled absently, and I thought I knew what he meant. "Me and Lisa," he continued, "back before she forgot we were made for each other. We took this walk once on a wooden sidewalk over a Louisiana swamp, down where you can get grilled raccoons and all these half-Indian guys speak French. Boy, this really bummed her out. Maybe it's why she didn't love me anymore. I'd just been telling her about that pisses memory-bank concept when I stand up on the railing, and I'm pissing into the swamp while she's off looking at a sign that helps you name birds, when all of a sudden, this big alligator explodes out of the water right at me."

"You're kidding, right," I said. My body had begun to stiffen and sleep was very close.

"Nope, completely serious." He sat down again. "Gators lie underwater really asleep, waiting to rip up a deer or something, and their teeth are really blunt so when they bite they have to tear to cut things apart. They're attracted to any motion at all."

"So, what happened?"

"It just missed."

"Too bad."

"Yeah, not really though."

"Just for the story, but yeah."

"Lisa didn't believe it even happened. She never believed me about anything."

"Smart."

"Yeah." He pulled a dark watch cap low over his head, tucked his sleeping bag around his legs. "So, I was like, Okay, *you* try it. And you know what? She did. I tried to stop her, because she could've got killed, but she got up on that railing, and then she was yelling, 'Come on, you gators! *Eat me!*' "

"She said that?"

"She had a pretty dirty mouth."

"I like that."

"Me, too."

"So?"

"They did." He lay down now, his head on a sweater.

"Dude, what happened?"

"I guess she had to prove me wrong."

"Yeah?"

"Yep. ROAR!"

"The *alligator*? Is that true?"

He nodded, put his hands behind his head.

"That's a horrible story."

"I know, I know. But, wow. Those scaly green

jaws full of jagged teeth like exploding out of the swamp and slamming shut right under her . . . but, you're right. She fell off the railing with her pants down and kind of bruised her hip. Which did suck. She laughed about it later, but she said I never think about anybody but myself."

Very late that night, the wall seemed to have a gravity of its own the way MRI scanners apparently make all your hydrogen molecules stand up and shout *hello!*, and though I didn't dream at all, I woke up once on my floating coffin of a ledge surprised that I'd slept. The moon shone so bright I thought a rescue ranger had a flashlight in my eyes. The wall vanished utterly into the sky—my personal Pacific rolling above—such that all of space seemed to stop right here. The haul bag dangled like a white cross. Mo lay next to me, still unroped, most of his long body out of the sleeping bag. His sweater was pillowed beneath his head and his knees were up, lips working in a patient argument; trusting his unconscious not to provoke an untimely roll or lurch, not to take the waking life down forever into the vagaries of sleep.

Dawn came over Yosemite more as an ambient glowing of things than as a distinct astronomical fact. With El Capitan in shadow, the sun rose well out of sight. I opened my eyes and felt the wall push down inside me. As if in a giant prayer room, I opened my ears to the distant reaches of the Hall, thinking, *In all this space something must be stirring.* I tracked currents and eddies of silence into far-off rooms and mile-long corridors, held my breath to hear even the ghosts stirring between stones—the thump of my heart not a timbal in life's great rhythmic orchestra so much as a singular, unusual, tentative fact. My fingers had become pus sausages from all the hauling on ropes and from being crammed into cracks all day. A little electrolyte/carbohydrate drink helped the anti-inflammatory pills down. I settled back on my rancid sleeping bag and noticed that the whole chain of tendon and muscle from my calves to my neck had simul-cramped overnight.

Mo rubbed his eyes with the heel of his palm, not wanting those foul fingertips anywhere near a mucous membrane. "Funny it's Friday, huh?" he asked.

"Hm?"

"Well, tomorrow's Saturday and we'll just sleep up here again, and then Sunday?"

"Heavy, huh?"

"Maybe be on top by Monday?" A cool wind slipped along the stone, and dawn-shadows yawned off prows in thousand-foot arcs. We both felt too sick to eat much, so we just chewed at strawberry Pop-Tarts and gulped water. The raven floated into these middle realms of granite on an early thermal bubble, alighted nearby. With the fire exodus over, no cars moved on the Valley floor. The Captain's skyline ran clean and sweeping before the reddening eastern sky. Against it, I saw a curious thing. With no clouds in that limpid daylight, the first sliver of the sun's disk broke across the wall's vertical horizon, and some spiderlike rune burned in its very heart. I stood up from my sleeping bag to read that rune, touched Mo on the shoulder and pointed, trying to see what the hell it was. Magnified by the light behind, a climber moved silently in the distance. An oversize and stylized archetype of personal struggle, he had become a black antman suspended in a tumescent sun, lost in the journey of a lifetime. And even as we saw him, the sun slipped further into view, and he shrank again, and then he vanished in the blinding flood of day.

When we began climbing at last, inching upward like faithful animals, wind picked up from the west—Central Valley heat drawn through foothill canyons. The swallows too found us again, but seemed more benign. We ran our ropes quietly and efficiently, talking mostly in the querying voices of sleepy professors on a sunny afternoon. I felt good about life's outcome: all was fine, all part of a plan. Once, looking down a thousand feet and feeling the tension of my weight against my harness, I felt a murmuring queasiness. But I knew I would not fall. Chalk puffed like speck-angels into the air, catching the late morning light. At the edge of Lung Ledge, Mo lowered me on the rope and I ran sideways along the wall to reach the Hollow Flake, a massive slab of granite broken away from the wall. The route followed the fissure made by the flake's exfoliation, a crack that varied between six and ten inches wide—much too wide to jam hands securely into, not wide enough to accept one's body. There's nothing more miserable than climbing an off-width crack. You make upward progress by wedging one whole side of your body inside and performing painful contortions. Without going into a blow-by-blow, I'll just say that the Hollow Flake so cramped my muscles and tested my joints that I was reduced to uncensored screams of pain and full-body cold sweats of fear. At times, the contracting of virtually every muscle in my torso was all that kept me locked inside that awful thing; when I so much as exhaled, the drop in my chest volume caused me to slip.

Then Mo said something I didn't hear.

"Huh?"

"Howzit?"

"What!?"

"Interesting?"

I laughed at the bastard. "I'm interested."

"You're not bored?"

"Nope."

"Well, can I ask you something, then?"

"Mo! What do you think I'm doing up here?"

"I was just wondering if I could have your stuff?"

"WHAT!?"

"Like your stereo. If you die, I mean."

An hour later, hyperventilating from effort and fear, I pulled myself onto a ledge ten feet long and two feet wide. From a little accumulated white gravel grew a lonely sprig of grass. I sat a long time recovering. Then I hauled up that pig of a bag. Soon, Mo clambered after it. With the wind turning south, we ate more Pop-Tarts and gulped more water. Then Mo shouldered the hardware and pushed on. Dangling in the withering heat of the sun-fired white stone, I watched that Levi's-wearing battle wraith fight his way toward the Ear. Devolved in the UV bath of ozone-depleted altitudes as Mo approached the underside of that massive granite meat cleaver hanging like a lobe off the wall proper. A path from earth to heaven—a Yogic system, bona fide. Then Mo was out of sight behind the Ear. I could hear him struggling and panting as he turned himself around. With his back to the main wall, he bridged his legs across the thousand-foot drop to plant them on the inside of the dangling sheet of rock. Working his body sideways, Mo cried and whimpered the way I had on the Hollow Flake, playing it up for my benefit and enjoying the struggle. Lying in the midday heat with nothing to do but hold Mo's rope, I remembered a guy said to have been deep into a dangerous lead, dangling from iron skyhooks on a blank expanse while his belayer polluted himself with vodka below. The leader had paused in the beauty and horror to pull from his shorts a Penthouse centerfold and laminate it to an overhang with clear packing tape. With Mo in joyous agony overhead, strapped into his sit-harness and wrapped in loops of rope—bound by all the gear of the world's finest fetishists—I had a thought: "El Capitan." So named when a Cavalry captain—here to slaughter Indians—paused dumbstruck by the Big Stone's magnificence, certain he'd seen the work of God. Only a soldier could mistake this mistress for a captain! *La Capitane!*

"You awake down there?" Mo yelled from inside that frightening chasm.

"What?"

"Don't fall asleep on me, you bastard. This ain't easy."

"*La Patrona!*"

"What?"

"El Cap, man! My big, motherfucking *boss lady*!"

"What are you talking about?"

Soon I was on the ledge beside Mo, and we were thrashing around trying to organize our gear. Elated and optimistic, thrilled by the site of that glorious headwall hanging in the sky overhead, we laughed and chattered as we wrestled for position.

"No room for you here, bro."

"Cool, I'll just untie and jump off."

"Cool."

"Pretty bad idea, huh?"

"What, climbing?"

"Yeah, rock climbing. Pretty poor thinking, huh?"

"Shockingly bad judgment."

And then I dropped my knapsack.

Just like that.

It gave a graphic demonstration of gravity-plus-time, growing smaller by the second and then seeming to hang in some middle space without shrinking. Then it skipped off a slab and my blue rain jacket floated away like an amorphous glider. The specks of color vanished in trees that looked for all the world like tiny hedges.

"What was in there?" Mo inquired gently, peering down with a look of acute nausea.

Rain jacket. Long johns. Hat. The chameleon mountain skin without which I became man-minus-tools, a pink hairless ape with neither fur nor blubber. All of our lunch foods were gone, too. The sun hung low in a sky still quiet save for that southerly breeze. I looked the few hundred feet up toward the top of the free-hanging El Cap Spire, where we'd spend the night. Then I looked a thousand feet further into the remaining worlds of stone. If this wind became a storm, I would soak through in about five minutes, and die of hypothermia within an hour or two.

Mo looked like he'd just been expelled from school: pale, breathless, and dumbfounded. I was sure he wanted to scream at me.

"Mo."

He didn't answer.

"Mo, you know what this means?"

He shook his head as if fighting off tears, then looked away from me to the west, toward the sea.

"Mo, I'm going to have to go down."

"You can wear my rain gear. I won't need it."

I thought about this, guessed he could worry about his own skin if he wanted it that way. Then I thought better of it. "That's no good."

"I'm serious. I don't need it."

"But then *you* die, and I die because you die."

We couldn't possibly make all the rappels to the ground that late in the day, so we climbed up to the top of El Cap Spire just before dark. A truly wild bedroom, that shaft of stone the size of a grain silo had cracked away from the main wall and had a large and perfectly flat summit. We didn't talk much. I was embarrassed and angry and wondering how the hell I could go home if I didn't finish this. It seemed of a piece with everything else happening lately. Mo smoked a cigarette I didn't realize he'd brought, and untied to walk around. I begged him to stay tied in, but he wouldn't pay attention to me. Over the low-grade hum of abject background fear, distinct columns of fire smoke loomed vaguely in the distance. Water-bomber prop planes lumbered through the air. The sun spread a last dirty orange blaze through the western sky. We took a long time with our housekeeping that evening, and ate canned pastas—two each, to heal our bruised souls. We wouldn't need them anymore, anyway. We also opened two tins of sliced peaches, which seemed like the sweetest, slipperiest, happiest food imaginable. It was a little hard to believe any fingers were clean enough to eat with, so we tried to pour food right out of the cans, into our mouths.

Neither of us could speak to the other, and we took turns looking down. Sixteen rappels awaited us—almost two thousand feet of straight descent. Nothing safe about that at all.

"Mo," I said. "I'm sorry."

"Whatever. Your call."

"That's great."

"What am I supposed to say? I told you I'd give you my jacket. We've got two body bags we can cut up if we need it. And it's not going to rain anyway."

This was it—the inevitable moment between us, when Mo was willing to risk everything and when a voice inside me insisted that nothing was worth death. I absolutely ached to let go, to be as confident and careless as Mo, but I couldn't. I didn't want to tempt fate that way—I wanted the risks to be no more than the ones I'd signed up for. "I don't want to die, Mo."

"Relax, Ray."

Like it couldn't happen. Like nothing could happen, ever, to anyone. As if we weren't just flesh and blood on a glob of stone—as if whatever yarn Mo was living were security enough for both of us. "I can't relax, Mo."

"You still pretty bummed at me? About your book and all?"

I hadn't thought about it in a while, and was surprised to hear Mo bring it up. Of course I was still pretty confused, but my sense of shame and my fear of death were also making me resent Mo's serene courage. "Your dad called me a thief."

"I don't know about that, Ray."

"What's not to know?"

Mo looked into the smoky night. He rubbed his face with those big hands. "It was pretty hard for me to read that stuff, Ray. I even saw some of my own thought patterns in there. It was almost scary. It's like I have to watch myself thinking now."

"For Christ's sake, Mo."

"And why'd I have to hear about it from my dad, anyway?"

I was breathing hard and fast, and if I could turn time back to right then, and do things differently, I would. But I can't. "Your dad," I said, watching Mo's eyes become intent, waiting, "I hate that motherfucker. I really do. He's a mean piece of shit."

Mo's eyes got even wider and his jaw tightened, and I realized too late that I'd crossed an irretrievable moment in time, that I'd spoken unforgivably.

"I mean," I said, grasping, "I don't think you care about any of this anyway, because I don't think it's in your nature to take things away from people. Right?"

He sighed heavily. "Let's just go down in the morning, huh?"

"But you know what I mean?"

"Ray . . ." He seemed to search for words.

"What?"

"Nothing."

"Tell me."

"I don't want to."

Without another word, we moved as far apart as that little platform would allow, and lay down. I didn't sleep much, and I'm sure Mo didn't either.

We just lay for hours staring into the darkness, feeling each other's presence. I felt absolutely awful, furious at Mo and furious at myself. Very late that night, I noticed something unnerving: no stars, which could only mean clouds. We really should go down. I got out of my bag and walked to the obvious toilet, stood in the swimming darkness whereupon to piss into the absolute abyss of creation. Wondered if a storm was really coming. That giant wall exerted a strange gravity at my back, and Mo lay sleeping beside me. We were so goddamn close. We'd come all the way to Yosemite, found each other, gotten halfway up this great climb after so many years of dreaming about it, and we'd almost made it—we'd almost kept our mouths shut and snuck through to a happy ending. I took in the sky's blackness and tried to breathe. A few little lights shone in the distance. Me and my boy, hanging there in space, with no world above and no world below, no past and no future—still alone, after all, in perfect meaning well into the ether.

"Mo."

No answer.

"Mo."

"Mm?" He sat up in his sleeping bag.

"Is it any coincidence that Golden Gate Bridge suicides always jump facing the city, never the sea? Aside from the parking being more convenient on that side?"

"What are you talking about?" He sounded very, very agitated.

"Let's not go down."

"What?"

"I can't go down."

Mo rubbed his face in the darkness.

"I'm not kidding."

"Are you crying?" he asked.

I guessed I was.

"You don't think we ate too much food to-night?"

"Not if we're careful, and we make good time."

"I think we ate too much. We'll run out."

"No we won't. We'll be okay."

He paused. "Okay."

"Really? You mean that?"

"Oh, Ray." He shook his head. "Yeah, really."

I let out an anxious shout, a little band of vibed air rippling the night.

At midmorning, just below the monstrous roof that led to the final headwall, I climbed over a loose block the size of a truck engine. I felt sure it would break free and give me a Doctor Strangelove ride to the Valley floor. I looked down at my speck of a truck, at a few dot people in the meadow, and at the sad choreography of all those black cranes tiny on the river, rising and swirling, floating off the earth as a group. Lifting over the dead meadows and tall trees, they rode a current along the Cathedral Spires, over those broken buttresses and on to the Valley rim. Bound for some place far south, they swirled and rose like a party of souls en route to a different world. Then I saw why: the smoke had obscured an approaching storm. A translucent gray curtain of rain washed through the fire haze down-valley, and a ten-mile rain-beard answered the smoke jumpers' prayers. It moved not in drops or showers but in sheets shadowing whole mountainsides. I was only thirty feet below that big roof, so I climbed toward it. Just as the veil of water was so close I could taste it, I pulled underneath. No ledge to stand on, so I stuffed three friends beneath the roof, clipped slings through them, and anchored dangling there. Soon, lines of rain poured silently past. With no pavement to puddle in and no puddle to slap, the perfect spheres fell steadily by and disappeared below. The completely soundless downpour had the ethereal softness of heavy snowfall, as though water and earth were of such different substance that their collision never accrued meaning.

Mo dragged himself up to me, soaked through. We hung squashed together in quiet cogitation and welling fear. Odd to see a storm from so near its source, to see water seep out of clouds closer overhead than the ground was below. Mo had an extra sweater that would keep me warm as long as I stayed dry. We pulled out those morbid Vietnam vintage body bags, which had a creepy plastic smell. Not much to do besides pull mine around me like a Ziploc over a chicken thigh and to feel harness straps dig into my legs, to mutter speculations about the future and yearn for security and human warmth. Make banal observations about the immense value of things like soft-boiled eggs and sushi and hot sake. We hung all the rest of that day, muttering in chorus, "Rain, rain, go away, come again another day." In a windless downpour, without shadows or sunbeams or a changing sky, dusk came on as had dawn, in an imperceptible and perfectly uniform lessening of light. No vanishing source or burning alpenglow, just a fading out of the world as though it were nothing more substantial than light. The stirrups and harnesses became nearly unbearable, and we took a long time rigging nylon sacks into hammocklike seats. When it was dark, we opened canned minestrone soup and ate it slowly. Then we shared a liter of Burgundy. Soon, it became too cold to do anything at all. You'd expose a bit of skin and lose a bit of heat.

The acres of wet stone overhead drained down the wall until the roof's edge became a waterfall's lip. Big ribbons twisted before our eyes. On the Cathedral Rocks we could make out spraying funnels of foaming runoff. For most of that third day, we'd had the secret peace of the tropical waterfall cave, watching the shimmer from behind. By midnight, surface tension drew the spiraling streams along our dry ceiling. An inch at a time, our little haven shrank. My fingers and toes got increasingly cold and I shivered steadily.

The next morning, our hands were puffed to twice their normal size and coated with dirt-filled sores. By the end of the following day, we'd eaten our last few cookies—the very end of our food. We just waited and suffered in a Gordian tangle of rope and nylon, bound up and sweating. As I tried to sleep once again, I wondered if I was going to die there. For some reason, it no longer seemed so awful—probably because I knew what I was doing there, and which story I was living, and I believed in it. I even felt a little blessed for having reached such a stellar perch once in my short life. The south wind built in the cold hours of that afternoon. First its whisperings sounded like forewarning voices, and then the gusts became louder sucks and rents. Sweat condensed inside the body bag, even inside my clothing. Water found its way along the ropes and into our harnesses. Just before dark, a gust bounced us like ships dragging anchors in a gale. We could no longer keep the water out at all. Drops came hard across my face. I dozed once, only to awaken hyperventilating from cold.

"Mo," I said, thinking he couldn't possibly be asleep. "Mo." He didn't respond, so I pulled myself over and grabbed his shoulder.

He shook violently and his head snapped upright. "What?" he said in a panic. "What the hell?"

"You awake?" I asked.

"You can have my hat, or something. I'll be all right."

During a long silence, the wind became a breathless panting.

"I'm a little spooked."

Mo rubbed his face in the darkness. "Me too, huh? Pass the water." He honestly didn't sound worried.

A few lights came on below—a new firmament to replace the obscured one above. I could not stop shaking, and I worried that the ropes would freeze.

My fingers were thick and slow in the cold and I was unable to make a fist. Sometime that night, I turned on my headlamp to look at the anchor holding us to the wall. The very material correlative of faith and chance, it was just a few bits of steel, a few lumps of blacksmithery now playing the starring role in the Ray and Mo Death Drama. I could feel my weight in tension against it and had an unobstructed view into the blackness below. I thought of vanishing into the night sky, living for a time in a dream of black flight—past realms of shadowed stone, eyries and caverns and perches, perhaps soaring down toward the red blur of a fire truck hiding in the pit, away from the flames. Decided I wouldn't mind a cup of Earl Grey on a bright San Francisco morning on Fiona's porch with surf running high after a night of love and nothing to do but breathe and say thanks and kiss in nostalgia about that silly first night together. I imagined her agreeing to hike with me in some distant national park, or just to see a movie in the heart of a large city. Maybe a foreign film with a nihilistic message about human suffering. I pictured how I'd become too distracted by her lovely earlobes to pay any attention to the film, and she'd be irritated with me, but also delighted, and we'd leave the film early to go home together.

Near daybreak, I heard something through the hissing of the wind and rain slapping against the body bag. A voice.

"Did you hear that?" Mo asked, lifting his head again from its fetal huddle.

I had. A voice. A megaphone somewhere far below.

"CLIMBERS ON THE SALATHÉ," Yabber's
unmistakable voice said, apparently meaning us.
"RAISE ONE ARM IF YOU NEED A RESCUE.
RAISE TWO IF YOU DO NOT."

We held each other's gaze a long time, and Mo said, "I'll go down now, if you want." I remembered the last time, when there hadn't even been a storm, and I remembered the finality with which Mo had poured out all those water bottles. This time I was cold and weak and losing focus. We had no food left, and while I wasn't hypothermic yet, I would be. I imagined Yabber looking up through the crosshairs of that telescope. Muttering to Raffi perhaps: "Looks like Ray forgot his rain gear." A sinking weakness and sorrow came over me at the thought of leaving, both for the ignominy and failure and because I'd begun to love the way the world yawned away from us. It was as if we'd finally found that dwarfing perspective we'd always yearned for, that diving board in the heart of space. In the growing light, I could see the cluster of rescue personnel in the meadow now—a tiny group of colored specks. Off west, a charcoal-gray sky dumped a thick cloudburst into the foothills. I guessed they'd lower a few guys off the summit on thousand-foot ropes, bring us up that way. Looking at Mo, grizzled and bundled, I thought, *This is not my life. This is somebody else's life. Someone much stronger and cooler.* Mo looked at me in the coming light, and the rain on his face made a broad wash of tears.

The twenty-pound rack of hardware swung away from the wall in a gust, and ropes whipped into the sky like tentacles. If El Capitan was my ten-megaton Old Testament God, certainly I was humiliated and suffering before it. The dawn seemed very dark, and the air tasted like aluminum. Whenever the mist parted, we could see those men in the meadow, waiting to help us. By trading leads—taking turns at risk and groveling—we'd kept the whole thing a game played between only us. Now this third element—the elements themselves—forced our relative solitude upon us. Our water tasted of the plastic containers. Shreds of stormfog hung onto the Cathedral Spires like torn sails on broken masts. For a moment, a cloud descended over the Captain. We could see nothing beyond our disembodied rock drifting in the original mists: no sound, no sky, no earth, sun, shadow, or even darkness.

Mo and I looked at each other without speaking,

each waiting for the other to give in. Clouds rose as if on elevators, and raindrops passed through space from unknown origins to unknown ends.

"CLIMBERS ON THE SALATHÉ, RAISE ONE ARM IF YOU NEED A RESCUE, TWO IF YOU DO NOT."

What else could I do? I hated raising an arm, felt a petulant outrage at nothing in particular. Steam wisped off my ribs as I reached upwards.

Mo's eyebrows lifted. He looked at that one hand held in plain view of the men so far below.

Then Yabber called again. "ONE ARM FOR A RESCUE," he said, as if to make sure we'd heard him right. "TWO IF NOT."

I wiggled my cold toes in those resoled shoes, and with my free hand, I felt something in my pocket: those Jolly Ranchers. A few thousand calories, maybe. Little bits of sugar and sweetness and flavor and of Yabber's weird confidence. Mo was looking at me, waiting.

I raised the other arm.

Mo smiled wide and lifted both his arms into the air, too. We hung with wings spread for laughing flight, like stone angels adorning a grand natural cathedral.

The storm tasted like ocean, like fog and surf—washing us clean of sweat and blood and shit. As we ate through those Jolly Ranchers and got warmed by their little sucrose rushes, the meadow vanished and water blew sideways. I shook in hard spasms against my cutting harness, hyperventilating. Dripping loops of nylon tangled around my legs, and ropes slapped like guy lines in a sea gale. With sky and earth now immaterial in the storm, we might have been on an unformed planet whose waters had yet to gather and mountains had yet to rise. The gear glowed with electricity, and claps of thunder made the whole mountain tremble as if something much worse had happened, as if the wall had split in two or broken off. *Hail Mary, full of grace, the Lord is with thee, blessed art thou amongst women and blessed is the fruit of thy womb, Jesus, Holy Mary, mother of God, pray for us sinners, now and at the hour of our death, Amen.* For a while my mind ran to everything I'd miss—Evan's wedding and the soft pleasures of big cities and especially a love that might have been and which now, of course, seemed like guaranteed life-mate material. A gust took water straight up and blew Mo away from the wall as a sheet of electricity flashed like a door to another time. "Check it out, bro," Mo screeched in electrified blue flight. "I'm flying!" My own windy bouncing felt too much like falling for laughter to come easy, and I repeated under my breath, *I don't want to die, I don't want to die, I don't want to die.*

I worked at keeping that corpse sack around my shoulders and over my head for the interminable hours of that night. Rain lashed against it like pellets, and my wet feet lost feeling. At one point, Mo tried again to offer me his rain jacket, and in the lunacy of the gesture I realized he'd been making offers like that as long as I'd known him. He never felt that he had anything to lose, and so could let go, could always be the giving one and assume the world would take him where it needed him. It had always seemed so wasteful to me, risking everything just to maintain a childish openness. But in the misery of that storm, I felt the meaning to which Mo'd surrendered himself, the conviction that only in giving did you find out how little you had, and only then did you learn how little you were. *Please let this storm go away, please just forget about little old us and go rain somewhere else. Oh, yeah, and the wind. Any time we could have that wind stopped would be perfectly fine perfectly fine perfectly fine . . . ARRUUUGA! ARRUUUGA! THIS IS NOT A TEST!*—the whole storm and even the dark side of the earth either an unjust persecution of Mo Lehrman and Raymond Connelly (animated and labeled flesh pockets) personally, or just a case of tripping in nature's subway station and having the misfortune to fall in front of the Downtown Express. Which indeed it turned out to be, as my breath first became uncontrollably frantic with the shivers and then changed to an even calm. A warmth came to my skin from an unknown source. The passage of time and the passage of a life seemed less a tragedy than an acceptable, warm fact. Mo was already dreaming in that kind of sleep—exposed to the rain without moving much, mouth faintly blue and eyes not open, not fighting it. The bottom of Yosemite Valley seemed a lake of liquid stars, a heaven to fall down into, so I yielded to the long, warm exhaling—breathed out and out all my heat and air.

Mo nudged me awake at dawn the following day. I couldn't believe I'd only slept. The rain had stopped, and the Valley floor came and went beneath a shifting, swirling fleece of cloud. The air was poignant with the cool humidity of a world pausing to breathe. The clouds seemed less black, like sponges squeezed almost dry. A dream treat: no wind at all. Perfect stillness again.

"The proverbial abyss," Mo said.

"Mm . . . more like the actual one."

"Kind of scary, huh?"

"Yeah. Think we're going to live?"

"Oh, yeah."

"Yeah?"

"Yeah."

"Bacon, diet of the ancients?"

Layers of storm peeled off like smoke rings and drifted upwards, immersing us for a moment in fog and then vanishing into a thankful hole of blue in the sky.

Mo coughed slightly. "We need to move."

"Actually," I replied, "I've been thinking about our options myself, and down's out. So, I had a thought."

"Yeah?"

"Well, what about going *up*?"

"Hey, I trust your judgment."

The storm hadn't completely passed, but we did have to get going. Everything felt stiff and dangerous again as we unclipped from those bolts and shuffled toward motion. My hands were very tender as I unpeeled the corpse-covers and watched condensation steam off its black interiors, felt dampness in every inch of my body. A cool chill ran along my neck and spine. Arranging the sodden, triply heavy ropes to climb again, Mo demanded he get to lead out the giant roof to the overhang. After all that dangling and shivering, he wanted to climb. And then he was working his way under the roof, along a seam that ran to our right, clipping his stirrups into old pitons. Soon it became clear that the ropes were too wet to pull through the gear. Mo struggled with them a long time, halfway out that roof— thousands of feet above the ground. I could tell how exhausted he felt by the slow, deliberate nature of his movements.

He reached out behind his head and placed a piece on the first step of the roof itself. He clipped his stirrups to it, and let his weight come away from the wall. As he placed the next, I realized he didn't intend to run the rope through each piece of gear—facing the same predicament I had on the Hollow Flake, he risked a long fall in open sky. Mo's cheeks reddened as he pulled out enough rope to let him move forward. His suffering gave me no pleasure now. He swung and jerked slightly as he thrashed around, and his fingers didn't seem to be working right. Eventually, he found his rhythm and worked with an unhurried attention to detail. Soon he'd gained the roof's lip, and then he'd vanished from my sight—Nature's window cleaners, dangling in the wind-worlds of the upper atmosphere.

From somewhere above, I heard, "Hm."

"What?"

"Oh . . ."

"What?"

"Wow," he said, entirely to himself. A while later he seemed to remember me and said, "Yeah, nothing. Just pretty wild up here."

Half an hour later, the call came down: "I'm off."

"Belay off."

Then fifteen minutes later: "Rope's fixed."

"Thank you."

Ten minutes later: "Ready to haul."

When he'd brought the haul line taut against the bag's weight, I unclipped it from the anchor. It bristled with crushed water bottles like cheap Mardi Gras decorations. The haul line ran from the bag, up under the roof, and straight out around the ten-foot lip. When I let go of the bag, it swung nearly twenty feet away from me in a single rush of speed. Then it swung back in, and out again. Eventually, it began to jerk upwards. Because he'd placed no gear, the lead rope likewise ran straight between Mo and me with no attachment to the wall between. So I had to swing just like the bag, to cut loose from the anchor and fly away from the wall as if on a rope over a river. Bile came to my mouth as I spun and whirled. The walls of the Valley whipped past my eyes as I tried to get my ascenders in motion on the rope, tried to concentrate on simple, meaningful data only.

As I turned the roof myself, onto the final head-wall, the first sun in thirty-six hours hit that gently overhanging rampart of polished granite. Directly through the headwall ran a single crack—just enough to make ascent possible. On a gleaming shield in the sky, we had a view as if from the bottom of an airplane. Clouds hung like dancers after a ball, tired and aimless. One of the stoppers Mo had wedged in the crack refused to come out. I had to knock at it with the long, flat piece of metal we'd brought for the purpose. Then the stopper popped entirely out, and fell. It drifted down, and down, and then became too small for me to see. I fell asleep several times while hanging from the ropes, drifted to a far-off bonsai garden with Fiona beside me on a hand-carved cedar bench. I would have given a great deal for one last piece of candy.

"Mo, you got another Rancher?"

"Nada."

It could all have been the ramparts of heaven with Michelangelo's God-plus-man drifting past and Venus in a clamshell (wool-lined, perhaps) or maybe just the whole clam, or even some oysters. Raw would have been fine, but barbecued with cheap barbecue sauce would have been better, or maybe with butter and garlic and a little thyme like you'd get with Fiona at a bar in a November storm hammering Tomales Bay's sheet metal to an elegant ripple. Maybe with a beer and clam chowder, too, on the kind of brooding, drizzly afternoon that makes a contemplative lovers' weekend in a car on remote highways seem the finest, most melancholy form of eco-philia.

"Hey, Japhy." Mo dangled from the crack twenty feet overhead. He'd spoken softly.

"Mm?" Autumn, that was it. Autumn in the air.

"Whatcha doing?"

I hadn't moved in ten minutes. "Nothing. Just thinking about Tomales Bay. You ever been up there?"

He thought awhile, shifted his weight around at his anchor. "Yeah. It's pretty."

My life strained against my leg loops and waist belt, gravity right there in the flesh. The rope thinned under my weight, and I stared at the strand before my eyes—an expression of fate and faith. No swallows anywhere. Damp, metallic air and broken clouds. "They got oysters up there. Barbecued or raw. However you like them. I bet Fiona'd eat them barbecued."

"Not raw?"

"I don't think so."

"Why don't we finish the pitch, huh?"

I wouldn't have minded eating more than my share with maybe a little baked pheasant and winter vegetables followed by chocolate biscotti and liqueured coffee. Nor would I have minded forgetting that one fuck-up would send me falling for nearly *twenty seconds* before exploding in the talus.

"Hey, Mo. Think how long we'd fall right now, if we fell." One one-thousand, two one-thousand, three one-thousand, four one-thousand *Hey, there's the ledge we slept on last night!* seven one-thousand, eight one-thousand *And the place we got shit on!* ten one-thousand, eleven . . .

He laughed a sudden shouting guffaw and hung his head back to look at the clouds. "Pretty absurd for humans, huh?"

"Just dumb."

"Yeah. Poor thinking."

"Think we're having an actual experience?"

"You mean, like art where you could get hurt?"

The storm seemed to be swirling slowly, watching, deciding whether or not we'd had enough. The work had all the drama of replacing a carburetor—tie a knot, clip a biner, pull a rope, pull on rock, pull on gear, clip a biner or two and rearrange. Glinting fields of sculpted stone looked bright and freshly made, as if just brushed into form by a celestial putty knife. With only clouds above and below, the wall was like an asteroid in a galaxy of mist and light, a fairyland we'd snuck into through a hole in the sea. Amazing that the ordinary earth could be so far down and still connected to us. When the Valley floor became visible again, my itty-bitty pickup truck seemed smaller than a matchbox toy, just a dot of blue. People in the meadow were tiny flecks, like they must be to SEAL paratroopers toppling foreign emirates. I reached Mo, and I could see a dazed astonishment in his eyes. He didn't seem quite afraid, just open to the gravity and the religion. He was also very tired. He passed me the gear I'd need for the next lead, then lowered his head to nap while I got organized. His hands were bloody and almost entirely black with filth. He'd pulled his wool cap to just above his eyes.

"You looked in the mirror lately?" I asked.

"Why?"

"You look like awful."

I could see the little platform of the spire straight below and, farther still, the sweeping Heart Ledge. Taking the next lead, with the galactic auditorium yawning at my back, I had chores to do. Look overhead at the crack, gauge its width and shape, select something appropriate from the mass of hardware at my side. Then reach up, fit the unit into the crack, jerk it snug. Clip a stirrup to it, work a foot into the stirrup, then, holding the unit close with both hands, haul my body up until my waist came even with the unit. Place my waist hook and sit.

When I pulled onto Long Ledge—our final resting place—I stumbled along that rock catwalk to the old anchor bolts. There, I found a plastic bag containing a note.

"Sorry," the scrawled little letter read, "we didn't know you were there." Also inside were gifts whose value the givers could never have dreamed: a can of tuna, a box of Lemonhead candies, a joint, and four strike-anywhere matches. The bombers were definitely forgiven their heinous crime. When I'd hauled in the bag and Mo'd joined me on the ledge, I showed him the food.

Mo raised his eyebrows, seemed to think very hard about something. Then he nodded as if he'd reached a conclusion: "It's a good thing those guys shit on us."

"Probably saved our lives."

"Howbout that, huh?"

"Yeah, that was good shit."

We were both delirious, so we got a gigantic kick out of that remark and laughed ourselves into hurting. Mo did the honors of opening the can of tuna, revealing our last supper. We ate slowly and carefully, and then we each licked out exactly one half of the residual vegetable oil. We even divvied up the Lemonheads. Our patch of earth had begun reeling away from its sun, so we pulled out wet sleeping bags and both tied many knots—even Mo—agreeing in advance, with a handshake, to touch none of them after that first hit of weed. Then we listened to the mute THC muse in the cooling afternoon light. That last sunset was like the dateline: tomorrow, life would begin again and our truce would weaken. But for now, the wall was just a planet-sized ship's prow cleaving through time. When night finally fell, the stars—free of smoke and mist—were dazzling and profligate. I dreamt my first dream in a week, and it was just love on white couches in sun-flooded seaside rooms with billowing curtains and fresh guacamole.

That last morning, we woke up filthy, swollen, sore, and witness to the first true autumn day of the year: the air still and cold, a faint snow dusting the meadows below, and the storm clouds vanished like Raffi's coverings pulled back from the soul. Those cranes were long gone—soaring somewhere before the southward marching storm. With the summit attainable even in our low-glycogen, high-lactic-acid state of dispassionate unconcern, we lingered to let things dry in the sun. My fingers were disastrous: every cuticle torn off, every finger hang-nailed, joints rigid, gangrenous kielbasas absolutely unclenchable. I'd slept all night with them out of my bag. My whole body felt cramped, too, like a single pulled muscle with no point superior to any other, a sensory clarity devoid of anal or phallic cathexis, a body transfigured. The storm had cleared most of the fire smoke, and only smoldering little columns warbled lazily toward the sun. One swallow fell cheerfully past, dropping off the world above rather than surging up from the one below. Samtanarasa, and we certainly risked falling both materially back to splatter and figuratively back to suffer in the material plane. Homeostatic nirvana, meditating on nothing. It took Mo a long time to get over his weed-bleariness, and we sat on that ledge for hours. I felt close to Mo just then, to his endlessly cheerful strength and even to whatever part of him would now keep me outside. With my toes over the abyss and my body deeply still—inert, even—I suffered in blissful attunement and atonement and smoked the last little bit of that joint. Watched a hunting peregrine falcon soar by at a hundred miles per hour, like the starship *Enterprise* looking for Klingon sparrows to dismember midflight.

The skies were so clear that the world seemed for once a manageable universe, my own Pueblo sandpainting writ large. The way those first astronauts wept at our small blue planet's beauty, I saw at last a bonsai California. From this diamond in the spine of the state, the golden sky poured westward across

California's Kansas, eddied among the hot and quiet coastal range, and gushed through redwood canyons to the kelpy sea, all from this center I'd defined by a jar on a hill—Sierra my soul's axis, and that home in the fog awaiting far beyond. Hot granite warmed inner ligaments and even bone marrow, and wet clothes steamed where we'd spread them out to dry. Ate a last Lemonhead. Saw a butterfly and a little grass in the cracks indicating the proximity of the top—botany, as encouraging as a shorebird would be to an ocean castaway. Eventually felt dry through and through, stood with shirt off on the ledge and walked up and down, feeling reborn. Saw clearly crystals in the granite that I'd always known were there but had needed four days of constant scrutiny and the spaciness of this complete yang deficit to truly appreciate—salt-and-pepper scatterings of feldspar, hornblende, and mica bonded at the earth's core, the billions of little parts making the whole, the whole maybe, just maybe, big enough to actually count. The body needs catatonic exhaustion from worthy means to feel free and pure, and a little ibuprofen is immensely helpful.

I woke from a nap to see Mo packing the haul bag. It was noon and we hadn't moved.

"Kinda hate to leave," Mo said.

Mm.

"Also kind of dying to get out of here."

Mm. Strange to be at last an agent of my own destiny, to become as a child up here, sucking my thumb. I'd craved this day for so long, had spent so many nights dreaming of it with this very man, and now it was so undeniably sad. I also noticed that Mo had left our traditional celebratory bottle of summit wine out of the haul bag, sitting on the ledge. I asked what was up.

"Just seems like we ought to leave it here, doesn't it?"

"Why?"

"I don't know. Just seems like we should leave something."

I am a climber, I am an American, I am a stool-eating hog.

While none of it could be helped, I climbed slowly to savor the firm concretion of that bright white granite and the tacit commands Mo and I now barely had to voice to each other: *On belay? Yeah, you're on. Climbing.* A double rainbow splashed over the now-visible Sierra highcountry, over distant saw-toothed ridgelines shimmering with the early snow. As we climbed, the sun warmed the stone and I wanted to linger, to savor the joys of being connected by a rope, and of living with a clear mission and no history. It all seemed so familiar now, the known world. The filth and suffering would soon recede, and the larger world would remind us of other people we were and of all the things between us. I led a last body-width crack observed only by a blue moth. Felt weak and dispassionate. Certainly the need for vigilance lingered.

"Boy, let's not blow it now, huh?"

"No kidding. Check your belay."

"Yeah."

Mo let me lead the last pitch to the summit. He knew summits were my problem, not his. At around two o'clock I pulled lazily up the last crack Mo and I would ever climb together. Sank hands deep into the stone, fattened them out, shoved feet in the crack, and pulled up. Move after move. Then slapped a hand onto flat rock, and pulled over the top of the Big Stone.

Funny, too, because there were a few small pines and shrubs there, and the earth sloped gently up toward a forest. A red butterfly sat on a black boulder.

When Mo had followed, he stumbled away from the edge and mumbled something in surprise at a solitary crimson columbine dangling its ovaries like a bloody ballroom chandelier.

"Hm?"

"No top," he said. The filthy, sodden cord lay between us, dead on the ground.

"No top?" I looked around again and realized that was exactly what had struck me. El Cap is really a cliff, not a tower, so it doesn't have a proper summit. It doesn't end in any special world of stone or light. It just left us sprawling in the dirt under a tree on a sunny afternoon while a beggar of a squirrel moved in on our empty cans. The dirt trail back to the meadow passed through bushes nearby.

"Amazing," Mo said, delighted by this geographical peculiarity. He sat heavily on a slab, looked at the little white fir I'd tied us into, and laughed in the heat. "I can't believe it." He grinned in childlike joy from his new crow's feet to the upturned corners of his huge, friendly mouth. "We're just back on the ground." And of course it was true. No top, and no more journey.

A small man, like I said, Evan had thickly muscled legs and arms and loved grooming the beast into submission: colognes, filed fingernails, undressed for success in designer briefs and matching undershirt. An autumn breeze brushed seaward while we donned ludicrous British Country Squire tuxedo getups. ("Actually," Evan had said, "they're cutaways. You never wear a tuxedo before five.") We'd already been through all the last-minute psychotherapy about whether marriage was a good idea, what I should do if his mother-in-law became difficult, and why I'd have to forgive his bride's outrage with me—I had, after all, seduced him into a truly hazardous hallucinogenic journey only two weeks before their wedding day. We'd also talked over the post-ceremony delivery of his getaway car, and even the birdseed for tossing. Evan's possessions were packed and boxed, ready for the big cohabitation, and my obsolete photo of El Cap hung alone on the living room wall. We were held up only by the groom's need, on this-his-wedding day, to transform his Cookie Monster monobrow into something like distinct eyebrows. While he worked, I sat on his brass bed and sipped Earl Grey, nibbled at a slightly burnt English muffin and its underboiled egg.

As Evan brought his gold-handled razor down through the fine fuzz on his forehead, I picked up the *San Francisco Chronicle* and read that they'd tracked the harbor dismemberer to a particular paint factory via traces on those buckets. Turned out the guy'd knocked up his mistress, flipped when she threatened to expose him, dosed on angel dust, and cut her to pieces. Dumped those buckets while on a family trip to the beach. In other news, a Michigan senator had been accused of groping a fifteen-year-old summer intern, a Jersey carpet salesman had been beheaded by a faulty elevator, and still I had the brain-swimming-in-love-honey feeling that a quick return to sea level often produces in the altitude-acclimated. Enjoyed the release from all-consuming pain and the sense of being comfortably ensconced in the denouement of an adequate story and unaware of even the premise—much less the crisis—of the next. All those milk crates full of hardware and tape-armored Coke bottles and badly coiled ropes, now in my custody alone, were welcome to spend a few days on my bedroom floor awaiting my attentions. In spite of needing to look for a job, and despite having read how the carpet salesman's appalled co-workers had been trapped for two hours in the broken elevator with his blood-spouting, headless body—like those mannequins at the Industrial Fright and Damage show—I felt overcome with an effusing warmth toward everyone and everything around me. I even had the courage to pick up Fiona's letter again.

"Raymond," Evan said. "How many times you going to read that thing?"

"You really think she means the Sierra de La Laguna? Outside Todos?"

"Of course she does. There's lots of little towns in those mountains that could use a church. You got to take a road trip."

" 'I just wanted you to know I liked meeting you,' " I read aloud. "Liked meeting me? What the hell's that?"

"It's just what it sounds like. She liked meeting you. We've been over this. She wouldn't have put in the part about feeling close to you if she never wanted to see you again."

"But why wouldn't she just say that?"

"Enough about *your* love life, Ray. Come help me with my face." He leaned over and rinsed off. Suddenly, Evan had brows where once he'd had a brow. They were spaced exactly the width of his razor, and a little unevenly, making him look drunk. I told Evan to take a little more off the inside of the right brow, but not too much. Then he rubbed mousse through his hair and said, "My *stylist* gave me this special little tip. Latin man name Jorge, say, 'You balding, so, leetle cream, very careful, you look very good.' "

"You do look good."

"You're right, I do."

"All ready, huh?"

"Yep."

"You love her?"

"Yep."

I pulled Evan's bow tie straight.

My groomsman's outfit hung off me like drapery. You feel heroic after a big wall, but you look more like a cerebral malaria survivor who's been jumped by an L.A. street gang. I'd lost twenty-five pounds and hadn't fully recovered, despite the fact that the whole drive home was a sequence of lard-stops. The morning after our long stumble back down to the Valley floor, Mo and I'd gorged on sausage and eggs and French toast and bacon. Vicky was working, and she was very happy for us, if only because she knew about the time I'd chickened out. We weren't stars or even veterans by Yosemite standards anyway, and we'd brought no fire back from the Gods, destroyed no death star. We'd returned with nothing more than some private glow of our own, and would give to the world only whatever tiny benefit might derive from our being slightly better-adjusted participants in its daily machinations. In the parking lot, we sat on the tailgate in the warm autumn sun and looked aimlessly into the empty Camp Four, feeling truly a part of it only on our way out. Raffi's van was all locked up, and Yabber's was gone altogether. We made a last stop to walk the wall's base collecting shit bags, which lay in the trees like moon rocks in some Australian farmer's field. The grim chore had a kind of moral correctness to it, a karmic balancing.

Heading home, with Mo's feet up on that dashboard where Fiona's had been, I drove very slowly and we didn't talk at all. Dropping out of the mountains, we passed incinerated forest holocausts and weary fire crews, waved at that kindly old Yosemite Indian ranger at the park gate. Past the sweet river swimming hole, I thought of Evan and the circling vulture, and was glad to be bringing Mo to the wedding. We wound among those ranches with their gory freezers, right by the sleepy Kiwi Tavern and its now-traceless gravel pile, and eventually into the sprawling cow town of Oakdale. After Oakdale, those ruler-straight highways run through Central Valley farms to Manteca, and then onto the big freeways. So we sat awhile in Oakdale's country highway sunshine, delayed our re-entry. Among tractors and tract homes we found an old rodeo grounds. We bought Cokes and watched cowboys work on their bull riding with the smell of oncoming winter tinting the air. Now I wish we hadn't made that stop, because when I finally said we ought to get on home for that wedding, Mo surprised me. He wanted me to leave him at the Oakdale Greyhound Station. At first, he wouldn't say where he was going. I tried to argue— told him how much Evan wanted him to be there, and how he could stay at my place if he didn't want to deal with the warehouse. But I was just talking to myself, and I knew it. Mo had his mind made up. Whatever journey he was on, he'd decided somewhere along the line that the Big Stone hadn't finished it, and that I wasn't its proper companion. Both were true.

I stuck around while he waited for a bus, and ordered him a double-bacon cheeseburger lunch and a real ice-cream shake with fresh bananas. For a while, we didn't talk about anything important. I guess the ridiculous things I'd said about his dad were in the air, and also the way everything was still unresolved. People in the diner looked curiously at us as we played the Galaga video game—so filthy, gaunt, and scabbed, and with a faraway look in our eyes. When the food came, I felt pure presence there in that white room at that red table, eating and watching a golf tournament on TV. We talked a little about where Mo might go, and I sat across from his broad face, knowing I wouldn't see it for a long time. I tried to picture it in twenty years— tried to picture myself. Thought about that particular smile of his, and his loping walk ahead of me on the midnight path to the wall.

"Thank you," I said abruptly.

"For what?"

"For getting me up that thing, I mean. And all of it."

"Come on, Ray."

His bus's engine kicked on—bound for Washington State, where Mo knew a guy with a lakeside cabin. We stepped out to the sidewalk and stood in the late afternoon sun. The Sierra loomed like an oblong moon to the east. We hugged stiffly and congratulated each other, and then Mo walked toward his bus. I'd watched his back that way so many times, but always while following him. About ten paces away, he stopped short and turned around. I could see how much weight he'd lost, and the low light etched out the bones of his nose and jaw. An Asian family was boarding the bus behind Mo, looking forlorn and committed. There were no clouds anywhere, and no agricultural haze.

"You know, Ray," Mo said, "you really did ruin those stories for me, okay?"

I nodded.

He rubbed his face and frowned, then glanced away. "But I don't really care about that anymore," he added, looking back. "You can have them, if you want."

I tried to smile.

Then Mo boarded the bus and I stepped back inside the station. I stood where I could see him through the waiting room glass. In his seat, Mo's head hung low, unaware of my gaze. His sunburnt cheeks and sad eyes were still so beautifully young and light. I knew we'd be strangers the next time we met.

As I drove the last leg home, I noticed that the fruit pickers had already gone south for the winter, probably harvesting oranges in the Imperial Valley. In fallow green fields, big harvesting gear stood idle. Boarded-up fruit stands threw long shadows, and the sky sparkled clear to Mount Diablo off west. After the mall sprawl of the Livermore Valley of Nuclear Death, beyond the whirring windmills and sluggish aqueducts of Altamont Pass, the road descended toward the great San Francisco Bay. At sunset, a blast of marine coolness brought eucalyptus and brine smells in the windows as the big bay spread all around with its lights and its vacuous watery blacknesses, its misty mountainscape islands darkening in the dusk and the red Pacific burning itself out far behind my lovely town—not a shred of fog anywhere as the clear autumn came on. By the time I punched through the Yerba Buena tunnel on the Bay Bridge and emerged shooting right at that most civilized of glittering downtowns, I was very glad to be home.

Now, as Evan and I arrived at a big Catholic church in Pacific Heights, dressed like a couple of cellists, all of San Francisco seemed etched in glass, washed clean by that storm and lit up by the fall sun. Inside the monstrous temple, I felt quite awkward, all tightened up in tails, being quickly briefed on my place on the altar, given a little index card for what to say when—not much, really. I actually took Communion that day, for the first time in ten years, and the wine tasted much like the Christian Brothers we'd left up on the wall. Throughout the endless, meandering ceremony, in which the priest got Evan's name wrong twice and I missed every sit-down stand-up cue, I passed the time by enjoying the architecture, rocking back on my patent-leather heels and deciding that all that time of all these people saying this place held God meant it held *some*thing worthwhile. Thought a bit about *The Torch and the Tulip*, and how the book ends with a huge wedding on the Torch's Georgia plantation, all the villains slain and the good friends watching. It occurred to me that I was just one of the Torch's good friends—an extra in a dime novel—and it felt great. Evan and his bride, a pale woman with an air of sturdy endurance, were bursting with affection and sweet desire for each other on the altar. They both wept with fear and elation when the priest told them to kiss, and it was a real honest-to-goodness tongue kiss, full of passion and hope. I don't know why, but it absolutely killed me, got me crying too as the ceremony ended. Tears kept coming down as all these beautiful choirboys crowded around the nuptial couple for photographs. As much of a turkey as Evan was for this phony vision of harmony and patriarchy, he'd built a life and declared a culture intact, and although the church was a factory (we were the third of five weddings that day), it all still counted, was still marriage and love. The way I'd envied those Hare Krishnas, I began to envy Evan his pleasure in his job, his love for his bride, and his willingness to take the simplest of American dreams and declare it his own. Most of all, I envied the water on the priest's pale, bony fingers.

Todos Santos, B.C.S., 1997